SCANDALOUS BEHAVIOR

This Large Print Book carries the
Seal of Approval of N.A.V.H.

SCANDALOUS BEHAVIOR

STUART WOODS

LARGE PRINT PRESS
A part of Gale, Cengage Learning

GALE
CENGAGE Learning·

Farmington Hills, Mich • San Francisco • New York • Waterville, Maine
Meriden, Conn • Mason, Ohio • Chicago

GALE
CENGAGE Learning·

LIBRARY OF CONGRESS CATALOGING-IN-PUBLICATION DATA

Names: Woods, Stuart.
Title: Scandalous behavior / Stuart Woods.
Description: Large print edition. | Waterville, Maine : Thorndike Press, 2016. | © 2016 | Series: A Stone Barrington novel | Series: Thorndike Press large print basic
Identifiers: LCCN 2015044691| ISBN 9781410480231 (hardback) | ISBN 1410480232 (hardcover)
Subjects: LCSH: Barrington, Stone (Fictitious character)—Fiction. | Private investigators—Fiction. | BISAC: FICTION / Thrillers. | GSAFD: Suspense fiction.
Classification: LCC PS3573.O642 S38 2016 | DDC 813/.54—dc23
LC record available at http://lccn.loc.gov/2015044691

ISBN 13: 978-1-59413-865-2 (pbk.)
ISBN 10: 1-59413-865-6 (pbk.)

Published in 2016 by arrangement with G. P. Putnam's Sons, an imprint of Penguin Publishing Group, a division of Penguin Random House LLC

Printed in the United States of America
1 2 3 4 5 6 7 20 19 18 17 16

SCANDALOUS BEHAVIOR

1

Stone landed his airplane at Southampton International Airport, in England, and taxied to the FBO, Signature Aviation. As he came to a halt and shut down his engines, an Aston Martin coupe drew up alongside the airplane, closely followed by a sinister-looking black Range Rover with darkened windows, as was Felicity's due as director of MI6, the British foreign intelligence service. As Stone opened the cabin door and came down the steps, Dame Felicity Devonshire got out of the Aston Martin and flung herself into his arms.

After a kiss and a hug, Stone stowed the cabin steps, closed and locked the door, and got his bags out of the forward luggage compartment. A man in a dark suit got out of the Range Rover, took his luggage, and stowed it in the SUV.

"What airplane is this?" Felicity asked.

"The new one: a Citation CJ3 Plus."

"I love the paint job."

"Thanks, it's my own. You can always spot me on a ramp by the stars on the tail." He walked around the car. "And what Aston Martin is this?"

"It's the DBS, brand-new. I recently sold my father's estate in Kent, so I splurged."

"You certainly did." Stone got into the passenger seat. "I should check in at the FBO."

"Don't bother, it's taken care of. They'll put it in the hangar straightaway and refuel it whenever you like."

"So what's the big surprise?"

"You'll have to wait a little while and take a boat ride, before all is revealed." She drove quickly out of town and onto a motorway for a short distance, which she covered in record time. Soon they were driving through the village of Beaulieu (pronounced "Bewley" in England), then down the eastern side of the Beaulieu River, a tidal estuary that flowed into the Solent, the body of water separating the Isle of Wight from the mainland. Soon she used a remote control to open a wrought-iron gate, hung on old stone pillars, and drove down a driveway lined with ancient trees until a large stone cottage with a slate roof revealed itself.

"Come with me," she said. "My housekeeper will take your bags upstairs and press your dinner suit." She led him through a handsomely decorated living room and out a rear door, and they walked down a stone path to a dock, where a charming old wooden cabin cruiser was moored. She got the engines started while Stone dealt with the lines, and they proceeded downstream half a mile and tied up at another dock, where a sign read: WINDWARD HALL. They walked up from the floating pontoon and were met by a man in an electric vehicle who took them down a shaded drive.

"Stop here, Stan," Felicity said. "Come on, Stone, we'll walk."

Stone got down from the cart and followed her farther along the narrow road. Without warning they emerged from the trees, and there before them, in a lovely meadow, dotted with old oaks and half a dozen grazing horses, was the most beautiful Georgian house Stone had ever seen. It was not overly large and it was symmetrical, with wings extending from either side. In the center was a white portico supported by four slender columns. Stone's breath was taken away. "I've never seen anything so perfect," he said.

"That was my reaction, too, when I first saw this house as a child. The owner was a friend of my father."

"Who lives here?"

"Sir Charles Bourne," she said. "Come, let's go inside."

"Is he expecting us?"

"He's in London this afternoon. He'll join us for dinner at the Royal Yacht Squadron in Cowes tonight, but someone else is expecting us." They walked up the steps, and the door was opened by a butler in his shirtsleeves and an apron, who stuffed a cleaning cloth into his pocket. "Hello, Geoffrey," she said. "This is Mr. Barrington. He's come to see the house."

"Of course, Dame Felicity," the man said in a beautifully modulated voice. "Ms. Blackburn is in the library. Shall I escort you?"

"No, Geoffrey, we'll find our way." They entered a central hall; the pictures had been removed, and scaffolding set up. "It's undergoing a major renovation, which is not yet quite done," she said, showing him a drawing room to his left and a library to his right, which had had all the books removed. "He's having many of the books rebound at a country bindery nearby, and the paneling sanded with two new coats of varnish. There are probably ten or twelve coats present already."

Another woman walked into the room, bearing a canvas carryall and a large drawing pad.

"Stone, this is Susan Blackburn, one of Britain's finest interior designers."

Stone took her hand. "I know your work from pictures in magazines," he said. "It's a pleasure."

"How do you do, Mr. Barrington?" she said coolly. She was tall, perhaps five-ten, and was wearing jeans and a chambray work shirt. Somehow, she made the clothes look elegant.

"Susan, will you show us what you're doing?"

"Of course." She walked them through the library and the drawing room, then took them to a lovely old kitchen with brand-new appliances, then upstairs and to the master suite, which was without furniture or curtains. "We've taken a small bedroom next door and turned it into a dressing room and bath, so there will be two of each. I think that arrangement preserves relationships."

"I agree," Stone said. "I have a similar arrangement in my New York house."

"There are four other bedrooms, each with en suite baths. The present house is the third on a very old property and was built in the 1920s. During the war, the RAF requisitioned it for a bomber base. They didn't give it up until the sixties. Sir Charles bought the place at that time and gave it a thorough systems upgrade, and all mod cons were installed, even air-conditioning. The house got pretty run-down and is now undergoing its first full renovation since that time." Some of the rooms were very nearly complete and Stone was impressed with the beauty of the fabrics and wallpapers the designer had employed. "The original estate was more than two thousand acres, in the eighteenth century, but now it's only around sixty. There are four cottages, a stable, and a greenhouse on the property."

They spent an hour seeing the house and the beautifully tended gardens. "The renovation is on schedule to be completed in six months' time," Susan said. "Sir Charles has moved into one of the cottages for the duration. Now, if you'll forgive me, I have to return to London for a meeting." She shook hands and departed.

"There's one more thing I want to show you," Felicity said. She took him back to the waiting cart, and they drove half a mile or so, through a grove of large trees, and emerged into a wide space bisected by a runway.

12

"I didn't know Brits had private airfields," Stone said.

"As Susan said, the RAF built it as a bomber base during the war, and Charles has maintained it as a fully functioning airfield. It even has a published GPS instrument approach, I'm told. Charles owned and flew a King Air, which he has recently sold."

"Is he getting too old to fly?"

"Too ill," Felicity said. "His doctors have given him only a few months to live. You wouldn't know it to see him, but he's really quite sick — his heart. They've told him that when the end comes, it will come quickly."

"I'm very sorry to hear that," Stone said. "It's sad that he won't get to enjoy the house when the work is complete."

"Yes, it is."

"Does he have family who will inherit?"

"He has a son and a daughter from whom he has been estranged for at least twenty years. Both are childless, and he won't leave the house to the National Trust, which he regards as some sort of communist institution that robs the wealthy of their property."

Stone waved a hand. "And this is your secret?"

"Not anymore."

13

"And why are you showing it to me?"
"Because I expect you to buy the place."

2

They sat, dressed for dinner, before a fire with a drink as the day waned. Stone had not reacted to Felicity's suggestion that he should buy the place, but while he was showering and dressing he could not think of anything else.

"Let me tell you all I know," Felicity said when they were settled.

"Please do."

"Charles has a very carefully thought-out plan: he and his children despise each other. There's no point in going into that history, but he says that if his son inherited, he would immediately apply for planning permission to build two hundred awful cottages on the property, and Charles won't have that. He says that his daughter would redecorate the house garishly and sell it to the first person to make a reasonable offer, without regard to what sort of person that might be. Charles, like many Englishmen of his generation and his class, has a long list of persons in mind who qualify as unsuitable, among them Arabs and Russians, who are driving the market in expensive properties these days. Fortunately, Beaulieu is too far from London to have attracted their attention.

"Charles knows that if he dies owning the house, no matter who he leaves it to, a battle will ensue between his children and the unfortunate inheritor. Therefore, he wants to sell it prior to his death to keep it out of their hands, retaining a lifetime tenancy. As I have pointed out, that will likely be no more than a few months.

"You have a number of qualities that would cause Charles to consider you an attractive buyer: One, he would prefer an American gentleman to an unsuitable English spiv — that is, a flashy person of dubious means — who, to Charles's way of thinking, doesn't deserve the money he has somehow made. Two, you are clearly a gentleman, one with an affinity for things English, who will turn up tonight in a dinner suit, instead of a boldly striped nightmare. Three, you are already a person of considerable property, which indicates to Charles that you know how to manage it. Four, you fly an airplane, and he would hate to see his airfield meet the plow. And five, you can write a check for the property, with no delays for obtaining financing or other burdensome requirements that give the opportunity for local gossip, which he has always despised. He would like to sell it as quietly as possible, then present his neighbors and his children with a fait accompli."

"And how large a check would Sir Charles expect me to write?"

"Ten million pounds, and let me remind you that the pound is down against the dollar. I need hardly tell you that that constitutes a screaming bargain in this market, especially with the fresh renovation."

"I should think he could get twice that," Stone observed.

"Yes, but you're not reckoning on Charles's way of calculating. What he wants is the house in proper hands, with the renovation and death duties paid and his loyal staff kept on, and a bit left over for distribution to a few charities he is fond of. Of course, he has other wealth — investments in stocks and business properties in London — but that doesn't come into the equation."

"How many staff?"

"A butler, a cook, and a property manager, and five others in the house, and eight or ten on the property — gardeners, stablemen, and laborers. He would like it if his horses lived out their lives on the estate, but he won't insist."

"Think about this carefully, Felicity, before you answer: Is there a catch in all this?"

Felicity laughed. "Two: his son and daughter will go out of their way to spread awful rumors about you, and you'll have to put up with me as a neighbor."

Stone laughed. "I think I can handle that."

"I'll defend you to the neighbors, and since I'm in London most of the time, anyway, I won't care who you sleep with. You'll have to buy me dinner now and then, though."

With the sun sinking, Felicity took them down the Beaulieu River and across the Solent. There was little wind, and the sea was calm. They fetched up at the little marina maintained by the Royal Yacht Squadron. A tall, slender man in a beautifully cut suit awaited them and helped Felicity ashore, while a uniformed boatman took their lines.

"Charles," Felicity said, "allow me to introduce you to Stone Barrington, of New York. Stone, this is Sir Charles Bourne."

Both men said, "How do you do," simultaneously, then they walked up the path to an old stone castle nestled close by the Solent. Sir Charles took them into a comfortable sitting room and rang for a steward, who took their drinks order. "Please give me a moment to change," Charles said. "I'm fresh off the ferry from Southampton." He vanished.

"Sir Charles seems to be everything he should be," Stone said.

"He thinks the same of you," Felicity replied. "I can tell. An upper-class English gentleman can feign a chilly warmth, but an Englishwoman will know the real thing when she sees it."

"This is quite a place," Stone said, looking around.

"The castle was built by Henry the Eighth, to repel the odious French, who never showed up. The Squadron is celebrating its bicentennial, having been founded in 1815, and is the second-oldest yacht club in the world, after the Royal Cork, which goes back to 1720. Sir Charles and I were practically born into it, both of us having fathers and grandfathers who were members. I was a Lady Associate member, until women were accepted as full members, and I became one of the first."

Sir Charles returned, dressed in a Squadron Mess Kit, in the naval style.

"Well, now, Mr. Barrington," he said, "are

you enjoying your stay in England?"

"Please, it's Stone, and I am very much enjoying my stay, although I arrived only this afternoon. I spent much of it enjoying your very beautiful property."

"I'm sorry it didn't greet you in its finished state, but we're getting there. Susan Blackburn is actually a bit ahead of schedule, but I'm sure something will go wrong to correct that."

"May I inquire about the origins of your title?" Stone asked.

"Oh, that arrived some thirty-odd years ago, at a time when I was giving rather too much money to the Conservative Party. Margaret Thatcher, who was a good friend, saw to it."

"Somehow, I had thought it more ancient."

"Like me, you mean?"

Stone smiled. "Hardly."

The steward appeared and announced dinner.

They dined in the Members Dining Room, the only people there, and they were surrounded by portraits of former commodores of the Squadron gazing down on them, some of whom were kings. The conversation flowed freely.

"It's nice that we have the place to ourselves," Sir Charles said, when their dishes had been taken away, to be replaced by port and Stilton. "It will be crowded at the weekend, and I'm happy to have had the opportunity to get to know you, Stone."

"Stone was very impressed with your property, Charles," Felicity said.

"Particularly the airfield," Stone said. He took his checkbook from his pocket and tore out one, already filled out. He signed it and handed it to Sir Charles. "I believe that is the correct amount?" he said.

Sir Charles put on his glasses and read the check carefully. "We have the same bank," he said, tucking the check into a pocket and offering his hand.

Stone shook it. "Please give me a week to move the funds from New York."

"Of course."

"In the meantime, a member of my law firm's London office will be in touch with your solicitor to prepare the necessary documents."

Sir Charles handed him two business cards. "One is mine, the other, my solicitor's. Will you be able to stay for the completion?"

"I'll call my office and see if they can spare me," Stone said.

They drank their port, then Sir Charles

changed back into his suit, and they returned to Felicity's boat. There was still a little light in the sky when they dropped off Sir Charles at his dock.

"Do you ride, Stone?" Bourne asked.

"Yes, Charles."

"Then why don't you wander over tomorrow morning, and I'll give you a tour of the property on horseback. Stay for lunch."

"I'd like that very much," Stone said, "but I don't have the clothes."

"I can help you with that," Felicity said.

"Ten o'clock, then?"

"I'll look forward to it."

They continued to Felicity's dock.

"That went awfully well," Felicity said as they walked up the path to her cottage. "Just as it should have gone."

"I am absolutely thrilled," Stone said. "Thank you so much for arranging everything so beautifully."

Then they went upstairs and went to bed, something to which they had both been looking forward.

3

The following morning Stone was wakened by Felicity for carnal purposes, then her housekeeper served them breakfast in bed.

"I'll get you some clothes," she said, when they were done. "You and my father are about the same size. What size boot do you wear?"

"Ten, American."

"That would be nine, British?"

"I believe so."

"Might work." She left the room and came back a few minutes later with a tweed jacket, a pair of whipcord riding trousers, boots, and a black cashmere turtleneck sweater. "I trust you have your own underwear," she said.

Stone got dressed, and everything worked. The boots might have been half a size large, but they would do.

"You may take the boat," Felicity said, "if you think you can handle it."

"I've something similar in Maine. I'll try not to wreck it."

"I'd better get you something water repellent, in case of rain," she said. "It sometimes happens in England." She found him a light Barbour jacket.

The morning was cloudless and the sun bright. Stone tied up at the Windward Hall dock, and Stan met him with the electric cart and drove him to the stables, where two horses had been saddled for them.

"Take the gelding," Charles said. "Name's Toff."

Stone slipped into his jacket, and they both mounted. Charles led the way for a short gallop, then Stone pulled alongside him and they continued at a walk.

"You've a good seat," Charles said.

"Thank you." Stone was remembering the last time he had ridden a horse. He and his son, Peter, and his girlfriend, Hattie, had left his wife, Arrington, at her new Virginia house and had taken the morning on horseback. When they returned to the house, they heard a noise like the wind slamming a heavy door, then saw a car drive away. When they entered the house they found Arrington dead in the foyer of a shotgun wound.

"Stone?"

"I'm sorry, I drifted away for a moment."

"An unpleasant memory, from the look on your face."

Stone nodded. "The day I lost my wife. That was the last time I was on a horse."

Charles nodded. "Do you have children?"

"A boy, in his mid-twenties. He's become a film director, in California."

"My son is a hedge fund manager, in London. Both he and his sister took after their mother. They seemed to regard me as an unpleasant, visiting stranger." He shrugged. "Perhaps I was that."

"Peter and I have a wonderful relationship. I don't see him often enough, since we're on opposite coasts."

Charles rode him past the row of cottages where some of the staff lived. "I've made that one my own," Charles said, pointing at a larger one set apart from the others in a grove of trees.

"What's the larger house over near the road?" Stone asked, pointing.

"That's the dower house, set apart for the widow of the lord of the manor. It's not included in the sale."

They rode on to the airfield, and Charles led him into a hangar with a gambrel roof and shingle siding. "What airplane do you fly?"

"A Citation CJ3 Plus."

"What's her wingspan?"

"Fifty-seven feet."

"Height of the tail?"

"Sixteen feet, I think."

"She'll be all right in here. There's a fuel truck out back that holds fifteen hundred gallons. Stan drives it over to the distributor and fills it, as needed. I get a wholesale price. I recently sold my King Air — can't pass the physical anymore. I managed to get a GPS approach authorized, which is useful, given the English weather."

"A very good idea."

"There are two fairly large airports, Southampton to the east and Bournemouth to the west, should you need repairs. There's a Citation Service Center in Doncaster, and they have one of those big trucks that makes house calls. They replaced an engine for me here, once, after Cessna bought Beechcraft and took over their servicing."

"That's good to know."

"I want you to know that all my people on the estate, both in the house and out, are first-rate. The most recent hire was ten years ago."

"I'll try to take good care of them. I like having horses about, too."

"They're good stock. Ride them as often

as you can. The girl groom exercises them daily. The old mare still has a few good years left in her, though I wouldn't run her much. The others are in prime condition. I've always held a gymkhana here in the autumn, to benefit the local SPCA, who do all the work of running it. Continuing it would stand you in good stead with the neighbors."

"I will do so."

They rode back to Charles's cottage, which Stone found well-furnished with his things. They had a meat pie and a salad and shared half a bottle of wine.

"How are you feeling these days?" Stone asked.

"Surprisingly well, as long as I don't exert myself too much. I've been offered a heart transplant, but I'll be eighty this year, so what's the point? I don't want to spend months in bed and more months in rehabilitation. I've had a good run and a fine life, and I don't want to spend my last years as a sick old man."

"I don't blame you. I hope you outlive your doctor's prediction. They're not always right, you know."

Charles smiled a little. "We shall see." He walked Stone to his horse and saw him mounted, then handed him his reins. "Will you give him back to the stables for me?"

"Of course."

"I see Susan Blackburn's car at the house. You met her, I take it?"

"I did."

"Fine figure of a woman. If I were a few years younger . . ."

"I'd like to go in and speak to her, if I may."

"Go right ahead. I've got some work to do here. We'll talk later."

Stone rode back to the stables, gave the horses to the groom, and went to the house. He found Susan Blackburn in the drawing room, hanging pictures.

"Good afternoon," she said.

He thought she looked very good in tight jeans and a sweater.

She read his mind. "You look pretty good in those riding pants, too."

Stone laughed.

"Did you have a good ride with Charles?"

"I did. He's doing all he can to help me acclimate."

"An amazing man," she said. "A wit like a carriage whip. He's got a woman in the village, you know, thirty years younger. She's his solicitor."

"I suppose I'll meet her when we complete the sale."

"No, that would be with his London

solicitor. Elizabeth handles his village business, mostly as an excuse to see each other. He's giving her the dower house, you know."

"We saw the house from a distance. He didn't mention Elizabeth."

"Oh, you'll meet her. They're an item around here. Have been for years. He was seeing her before his wife died, some years back. I don't think they had much of a marriage — too different. He moved into the cottage years ago."

"He thinks well of you," Stone said. "He's your admirer."

"Oh, I've seen that look in his eye."

"Are you taken?"

"I've been taken in my time," she said, laughing, "but at the moment I'm a free woman."

"I've got to go up to London in a day or two. May we have dinner?"

"I'd like that."

"May we go up and have another look at the master suite?"

"Of course. I can hang these pictures later. I've got some fabric samples to show you."

He followed her up the stairs, watching her ass all the way.

4

Susan showed him a swatch of antiqued leather. "I thought this for the sofa that was in the room."

"I like it," Stone said.

"The late Lady Bourne had turned this into a nest of Victorian frilliness, which made my skin crawl. I think, in view of the gender of the new owner, something a little more masculine would be better."

"I agree." Stone was standing next to a window, and something outside caught his eye. He squinted and saw a man in some sort of tattered cowl crossing the lawn, carrying a heavy staff. "Who do you suppose that is?" he asked Susan.

"Oh, that's just Wilfred, the hermit. He lives in a little hut in the woods that Charles built for him."

"A hermit?"

"A lot of the big estates had them in the past. It's supposed to be good luck to have a hermit living on the property. He doesn't bother anyone, and no one bothers him. I think he stops at the kitchen for food on a regular basis, though. Don't worry, he's harmless."

"If you say so," Stone said. "I'll look for him on the list of furnishings being conveyed."

"Speaking of furnishings, Charles has a rather nice art collection that I assume will come with the house. It's mostly middling stuff, chosen because Charles liked them, not for investment purposes. He does have a middling Constable, though — one of his many renderings of Salisbury Cathedral, and he has a very nice Turner. I've sent the best things out for cleaning and, in some cases, minor restoration. A lot of cigars have been smoked in this house over the decades, and smoke doesn't do much for pictures."

"Good." Stone looked at his watch. "It's time for me to make some calls to New York," he said. "Will you excuse me for a few minutes?"

"Of course."

Stone went into the dressing room, took out his iPhone, checked for a signal, and called the managing partner of Woodman & Weld, Bill Eggers.

"Are you back?" Eggers asked.

"Not yet. It'll be another week or so."

"Having fun?"

"Italy wasn't much fun. I'll tell you all about it when I get home."

"Where are you now?"

"In Hampshire, in England. God help me, Bill, I've bought another house."

"Good God."

"I'm going to balance things out, though, by selling you my house in Washington, Connecticut."

"I didn't even know you *had* a house in Washington, Connecticut, but I like the village very much. So does my wife."

"Run up there and have a look at it this weekend. Stay for a couple of nights. You'll love it. Joan will send over the keys and the security code."

"What the hell, all right. What do you want for it?"

"Don't worry, it'll be cheap, for Washington, Connecticut. I'll hold off listing it until I hear from you. In the meantime, will you call the London office and have them give me a bright young real estate lawyer to close this sale? Tell him to call me on my cell. I'm going up there in a day or two, and I'll want to see him."

"I'll take care of that now."

"See you next week sometime." He hung

up and called his broker, Ed.

"Good morning, Stone."

"Good afternoon. I'm in England, and I'm buying a house, so I have to move some money to my London account at Coutts & Company."

"How much do I have to shake loose?"

"Ten and a half million pounds, not dollars."

"Good, the pound is down against the dollar right now."

"I'll leave it to you which stocks to unload. Try not to make me any capital gains, though."

"All right, Stone, I'll get right on it. I'll want a written confirmation for this big a transfer, though."

"Will a handwritten note do?"

"That will be fine."

"Hang on a minute." He covered the phone and yelled, "Susan?"

"Yes?"

"Is there a working fax machine in the house?"

"Yes, down in the property manager's office."

"Okay, Ed, you'll have it in a few minutes. Start selling."

"Will do."

They both hung up, and Stone called Joan.

"Are you still in Rome?"

"No, now I'm in England for a week or so."

Joan sighed. "I suppose you're buying another house."

"How did you guess?"

"Oh, God, you don't mean it!"

"I'm afraid so. Don't worry, I'm going to sell the Washington, Connecticut, place to Bill Eggers."

"Has he agreed to buy it?"

"Not yet, but wait until he sees it."

"When are you coming home?"

"A week or so, don't rush me. Oh, will you go up to my dressing room and overnight me a couple of tweed jackets and my riding clothes and boots? I'm wearing borrowed clothes, and they stink of tobacco. Send them to the Connaught, in London. Mark the package 'Hold for arrival.' "

"Anything else?"

"Include another evening shirt and a couple of turtleneck sweaters, please."

"Right."

"See you next week, maybe late next week."

"Bye-bye."

He rejoined Susan. "Where will I find the fax machine?"

"I'll take you down and introduce you to

34

Major Bugg."

"He's the property manager?"

"Oh, yes, very much so. He's ex–Royal Marines."

Stone took the elevator down to the lower level of the house with her. "This is newly installed," she said.

"Good idea."

Major Bugg didn't snap to attention, but he did rise from his desk. He seemed in his mid-fifties, cropped gray hair, military mustache, three-piece tweed suit, gold watch chain. Susan introduced them.

"How do you do, Mr. Barrington?"

"Very well, thank you. I expect you and I should sit down and have a talk about the place later on, but right now I need to send a fax. May I have a sheet of the house letterhead, please?"

Bugg handed him a sheet, and he scrawled instructions to his broker, looked up the fax number on his iPhone, and Bugg sent it for him. He took care to retrieve the original note after it went through. "There," he said, "that's enough business for one day."

"I'll walk you out," Susan said, handing him a card. "My numbers in London."

Stone gave her his own card. "How about tomorrow evening?"

"That would be fine."

35

"I'm staying at the Connaught. May we meet in the bar there at, say, seven o'clock?"

"Yes, that would be convenient." She came with him to the front door, where Stan awaited with the cart.

"I'll look forward to seeing you in London."

"I, too," she said.

5

Felicity was returning to work the following morning, so he drove up to London with her in the Aston Martin.

"I think you should take out Susan Blackburn," she said as she whipped around a truck. "She's unattached, at the moment, I think, and you'll need to be entertained when I'm not around."

"I'll consider that," Stone replied.

"What do you have to do in London?"

"I'm lunching with my new attorney at the Reform Club to sign some documents that we discussed on the phone yesterday. I'll see my tailor and shirtmaker, and I suppose I'll need some transport, so I'll take a look at cars."

"Sounds like you have a full day."

"When will you return to Beaulieu?" he asked.

"Maybe this weekend — depends on work. The Middle East is a mess these days.

We should call it the Muddle East. I gave you a key, didn't I?"

"Yes, you did."

She dropped him at the Connaught, but his suite had not yet been vacated, and he was asked to come back after lunch. He walked up Mount Street to his tailor, Hayward, and ordered some suits, a tuxedo, and a reefer suit, which was a double-breasted blue suit with yacht club buttons. He also ordered an overcoat, in case he was at the house in winter. He would need clothes to fill his new dressing room at Windward Hall.

The Reform Club was a grand edifice in Pall Mall, whence Phileas Fogg had departed on his eighty-day wager around the world, both in the novel and in the film, which shot the opening scenes on-site. His attorney, whose name was Julian Whately, met him in the dining room. "Let's lunch first, then take our business to the library," Whately said. "We're not supposed to flash papers at table." They passed a pleasant lunch with Whately trying to explain cricket to him, and even after dessert, Stone still hadn't grasped either the rules or the point.

Ensconced in a corner of the magnificent library with coffee and papers, Whately produced a contract sent over by Sir Charles

Bourne's solicitors. "This is the most extraordinary thing I've ever seen," he said, handing it to Stone, "concerning a sale agreed at a first meeting. Virtually everything in the house included in the sale is listed — six or seven pages of it. They must have been working on it for weeks."

"Charles Bourne has known for weeks that he is dying," Stone said.

"Ah, that explains it. The only thing of note in the contract is that two paintings, a Constable and a Turner, are held out, but offered for separate purchase for two hundred thousand pounds. Are they worth it, do you know?"

"I'll find out at dinner," Stone said, signing both contracts, "and let you know in the morning. If not, you can burn that piece of paper."

"Do you have the funds ready?" Whately asked on the sidewalk while hailing a taxi.

"Yes, they're in the bank, and I've already given Bourne my personal check."

"Extraordinary," Whately said. "We can close whenever you and Sir Charles agree."

"Call his solicitor and tell him that. I'm headed back to Hampshire tomorrow, but I can stay, if he wants to close in London. Try for nine AM at the Connaught, in my suite."

"I'll let you know," Whately said. He got into the taxi and drove away.

Stone strolled up to Jermyn Street to his shirtmakers', Turnbull & Asser. He ordered two dozen shirts to be delivered to Windward Hall in four weeks, picked out a dozen neckties, and a couple of pairs of gloves, bought a dozen pairs of boxer shorts, half a dozen nightshirts, and a silk dressing gown, ordered them all sent to his hotel, then headed back to the Connaught on foot. He walked through the Burlington Arcade and found Anderson & Sheppard in Saville Row. He ordered two tweed jackets and some complementary trousers, then went on his way.

Then, in Berkeley Square, he came to the Bentley showroom and walked in.

A gleaming Flying Spur greeted him from a turntable, dark green metallic paint and Saffron leather. He watched it for two revolutions before a salesman materialized at his elbow.

"Shall I wrap it, sir, or will you drive it away?"

"How much?" Stone asked.

"I'm very much afraid this one has been sold. I've been waiting for ten days for the buyer to pay for it."

"Do you have anything else ready to go?"

"I'm afraid not, sir. It will take about three months to fill an order."

"Ah," Stone said, disappointed.

"Suppose my buyer backed out?" he asked. "Are you prepared to buy it now?"

Stone looked at the sticker on the window and came up with a figure fifteen percent less.

The salesman countered with ten percent.

"Done," Stone said.

"Will that be for export, sir?"

"No."

"Then we'll have to add Value Added Tax and car tax."

"Of course."

"One moment, sir." The man went to his desk and dialed a phone number. Stone caught snatches of his conversation. "Well, then, sir, we will refund your deposit immediately. Thank you for your custom." He hung up and returned to Stone's side. "I'm afraid the gentleman got caught a bit short," he said. "The car is yours."

They spent half an hour wading through the paperwork, then Stone wrote the man a check. "I'll pick it up at midday tomorrow," he said.

"Of course, Mr. Barrington. We will be ready for you."

Stone crossed Berkeley Square, passed

41

Annabel's, and then, at the end of the square, he spotted the Porsche showroom across the street. He went in and found a Carrera 4S, painted umber, with cognac leather, beckoning him. He checked the window sticker, but as a salesman detached himself from his chair and began coming toward him, Stone waved him away, then walked out and turned toward the Connaught.

"No," he said aloud to himself. "I can't buy a country estate, a Bentley, and a Porsche all in the same day." He arrived at the hotel and was led to his suite by a young assistant manager. The hotel had been sold and redecorated since he had last stayed there, and he didn't see a single familiar face among the staff. Still, he liked his suite.

He unpacked and turned on the TV, looking for some news, but he was distracted and could not concentrate on current events. Finally, he went downstairs, crossed the street, walked fifty meters, and bought the Porsche. He signed the documents, wrote a check, and asked the salesman to have it at the front door of the Connaught at ten AM the following morning, then he called the Bentley salesman and asked him to have the Flying Spur delivered to Windward Hall the following afternoon.

He walked back to the Connaught feeling a little lightheaded, but pleased with himself.

6

Stone was halfway through the potato chips on the bar by the time Susan walked in. He offered her a peck on the cheek, which was accepted, then sat her down at a table.

"I hope it wasn't inconvenient for us to meet here," he said, after he had ordered her a martini and himself a Knob Creek.

"Not in the least," she said. "I live in Farm Street, which is a stone's throw away and is reached from here by a very convenient footpath. How was your day?"

"Very good. I got quite a lot done."

"And what did you get done?"

"I lunched with my solicitor, then visited two tailors and my shirtmakers and made them all very happy, then I set about cheering up two automobile salesmen."

She laughed. "All these things for the new house, I assume."

"I'm starting from scratch."

"When do you complete the sale of the house?"

"Tomorrow morning at nine, here, in my suite."

"Which suite?"

He told her.

"I designed it."

"I rather thought you might have. It looks like you — cool, but with concealed warmth, and elegant. By the way, I have a question for you."

"Ask away."

"The two paintings — the middling Constable and the good Turner: Charles wants two hundred thousand pounds for them. Do you think that reasonable?"

"I would have thought it reasonable yesterday, when I described them to you in those terms, but this afternoon they were delivered to my office, and now, having been cleaned and reframed, the Constable is a very good example, and the Turner is spectacular. I should think they'd bring at least half again, perhaps twice that at auction."

"Then I will accept his offer."

"I will have two van loads of things going down to the house tomorrow, and I'll include the pictures, plus some others."

"Why don't you drive down with me tomorrow, if you're willing to put yourself in a car with a driver who is accustomed to driving on the right, not to say, the correct side of the road, and stay for a few days. You can even work, if you feel so inclined."

"Is that a business proposition or a personal one?"

"A little of both, but you may choose your sleeping quarters from the available stock. I think every designer should sleep in the room or rooms she has designed. How else can you know if you got it right?"

"A very good point. I'll think it over and give you an answer later in the evening. Where are we dining?"

"At Harry's Bar."

"Yum."

After the pasta course she assented to his invitation.

"What made you accept?" he asked.

"One martini and one glass of wine," she replied. "Also, I know something that you won't learn about until tomorrow morning."

"And what might that be?"

"Sir Charles, after having requested permission from the new owner of Windward, intends to throw a bash in the house on Sunday evening for forty or fifty of his most intimate friends, and he expects me to have the public rooms ready to receive them. So I will work while I'm there, along with the crews I'm sending down tomorrow, and I'll return to London on Monday morning."

"Perfect. And I will take off for New York on that day, too."

"How very convenient for us both."

Their osso buco arrived, and they returned their attentions to their food.

After dinner, Stone walked Susan to her house, in Farm Street. She did not invite him in. "It's rather a mess at the moment," she said, "and the cleaners won't be in until tomorrow."

"Then I will collect you a little after ten in the morning," Stone said. He kissed her on the lips, and she went inside, closing the door firmly behind her.

Sir Charles, his solicitor, and Julian Whately arrived together shortly after nine the following morning and were given coffee and pastries before the briefcases were unpacked and the paperwork for the closing on the sale of the house was stacked high on Stone's dining table, awaiting signatures.

"First," Stone said, handing Sir Charles a check, "I accept your offer of the two pictures, and Julian will give you the signed agreement."

"You are very welcome," Charles replied.

They began signing documents, and that took nearly forty-five minutes. "Congratulations," Sir Charles said, finally, "you are now the legal owner and lord of the manor of Windward Hall."

"Thank you," Stone replied, and the two men shook hands.

"Now, I have a request," Charles said. "On Sunday evening, may I host a party celebrating my eightieth birthday in the house?"

"Certainly, you may."

"Don't worry, I shall make all the arrangements and bear the cost."

"As you wish."

The two men shook hands, and they all traveled to the ground floor together, where Stone's new Porsche awaited, his luggage already aboard. They all shook hands again, and he drove around to Farm Street to collect Susan.

She had brought two large bags, and when he opened the boot, up front, he found it filled with his own things, and the space behind the front seats was taken up by the package Joan had sent him from New York and the things he had bought at Turnbull & Asser. "Don't worry," he said, placing Susan's two bags in her lap. "I have a solution."

He drove into Berkeley Square and around to the Bentley dealer. He got out of the Porsche, rapped on the window, and beckoned the salesman outside, then he unloaded the two cases from Susan's lap onto the sidewalk. "Will you kindly put these into the boot of the Bentley?" he asked.

"Of course, Mr. Barrington." He looked at his watch. "And I can have the car there by two o'clock."

"Perfect," Stone said. He got back into the Porsche. "When you're traveling in this car," he said to Susan, "you need a Bentley following you with the luggage."

"An excellent solution to our problem," she said. "And I can already feel the blood returning to my legs."

And so they set off for Windward Hall.

On the way out of London, clouds began to quickly gather, and by the time they were on the motorway, the downpour was so heavy that visibility was affected.

They arrived at Windward Hall — the first time Stone had entered the estate by the front gate — and as they approached the house in the still-steady rain they had to drive past a good-sized tent pitched on the lawn some twenty or thirty yards from the entrance to the house. Parked alongside the tent were two police cars, one unmarked, and an ambulance.

"What on earth is that?" Susan asked as they drove past.

"It appears to be a crime scene," Stone replied, "very likely a homicide."

7

Stone drove around the house to the court-
yard at the rear, which contained the stables
and garages, and drove into an open bay. As
they got out of the Porsche the butler,
Geoffrey, in his daytime apron and shirtsleeves, came out of the house and picked
up as many of Stone's bags as he could
carry, while Stone collected the rest. Geoffrey led them into the house through the
mudroom, which Stone figured would get
plenty of use today.

"What's happened out front of the
house?" he asked the butler, once they were
inside.

"A neighbor has been found, deceased, in
the meadow, and the police have questioned
all of the staff, one by one."

"Who is the neighbor?"

"Sir Richard Curtis, who lives at the
adjoining property to the south," Geoffrey
replied. "He was a very close friend of Sir

Charles."

"Has Sir Charles returned from London yet?"

"No, but he's expected in the early afternoon."

"Have you spoken with him about what's happened?"

"No, his mobile doesn't answer. Shall I put your things in the master suite?"

"Yes, please, in the dressing room — the old one, not the new one. Another car will be delivered this afternoon, and please see that it's parked in the garage and that Ms. Blackburn's bags are collected from the boot."

"Please put them in the Lilac Room," Susan said quickly, before Geoffrey could ask.

"Yes, madam," Geoffrey replied. "Would you and Ms. Blackburn like lunch?" he asked. "We've some hot soup and sandwiches."

"Yes, thank you. Perhaps in the library? Susan, is it fit for lunching?"

"I believe so," she said.

Geoffrey put Stone's things in the elevator and went upstairs.

"Do you know Sir Richard Curtis?" Stone asked Susan.

"No, I've never met him — never heard of

him, for that matter. It was inconsiderate of him, though, to die on your front lawn."

"From what we're hearing, it sounds as if he had help."

They went into the library, which seemed in good order, but dark. Susan opened the curtains on both sides of the fireplace and let in the gray light. "The room is missing only the Constable and the Turner, and those will be among the first items unloaded."

A woman came in with a tray and set a mahogany card table for lunch.

"Thank you, Elsie," Susan said. She lit the fire that had been laid, and in a moment a cheerful blaze was going. "It's nice to have a fire on a cold, rainy day," she said, backing up to it.

Stone came and warmed his hands. A moment later Elsie returned with a tray bearing a tureen and china and set the table further. "Luncheon is served, Mr. Barrington," she said. "Would you like wine?"

"A bottle of white burgundy would be good," Stone said, holding a chair for Susan, and Elsie disappeared.

He sat down and tried the soup. "Perfect," he said.

"Oh, Mrs. Whittle, Geoffrey's wife, has a reputation as the best cook in the county,"

Susan said. "Have you met her?"

"No, I have some catching up to do, in that regard." They finished their soup, and Elsie returned with their sandwiches and the wine. She uncorked it and gave Stone some to taste. "Excellent," he said, looking at the label. "A Batard-Montrachet," he said.

"Charles has an excellent cellar. Was it on the list of items conveyed with the house?"

"There was an item saying, 'the contents of the wine cellar, save two dozen bottles to be chosen by Sir Charles.' I thought that fair enough."

"I've noticed," Susan said, "that you speak English with an American accent, but with English phrasing. Is that deliberate?"

"No, I have an imitative ear, so I tend to speak my own language as the locals do, wherever I am. I came away from a week in Germany once, speaking broken English."

"That's a handy gift. It will make the locals here more comfortable with you. The British upper class tends to view Americans as noisy people with cameras, until they are shown something different. They will like you for your phraseology, because they will understand you the first time you say something."

"I draw the line at 'shedule' instead of

'skedule.' "

They were having coffee on a sofa before the fireplace when there was a sharp knock on the door. Stone turned to see a small man in a tweed suit, who was dabbing at his face with a handkerchief.

"Filthy weather," he said. "I beg your pardon, Mr. Barrington?"

Stone rose. "Yes."

"I am Deputy Chief Inspector Holmes," he said, "as in Sherlock."

"I hope that is not your Christian name," Stone said.

"Fortunately not, but I'm often called that anyway, by those who are out of reach of my authority."

"This is Ms. Susan Blackburn, who is the designer in charge of redoing the interior of the house."

"I would like to ask you a few questions, perhaps both of you."

"Of course, please sit."

Holmes took an armchair next to the sofa. "Damned good idea, a mudroom," he said, inspecting his shoes. "Saves tracking in the weather."

"We ran into the weather on the motorway," Stone said. "When did the rain start here?"

"Sometime last evening, according to the

staff. I'd like very much to know more precisely. It is my understanding that you are buying this property from Sir Charles Bourne."

"I bought it from him this morning, in London."

"He was there for the completion?"

"Yes."

"When did he come up to London?"

"I think yesterday sometime, but I'm not certain. It appears that we have a homicide on my front lawn."

Holmes looked at him sharply. "Why do you say that?"

"You've pitched a tent over the corpse to preserve the crime scene," Stone said. "And there are the vehicles."

"You're very observant," Holmes said.

"It was hard to miss, and I was once a homicide detective, in New York City."

"You were?" Susan asked, surprised.

"You were?" Holmes echoed.

"I was. Fourteen years on the NYPD, twelve of them in Homicide."

"You made detective in two years?"

"It was easier then. We had more than four thousand homicides in the city the year I was promoted, as compared to a little over three hundred last year. Somebody had to investigate them, and there weren't enough seasoned men per corpse."

"Quite," Holmes said.

Stone made a mental note not to say "quite" when speaking to Englishmen; they would think he was trying too hard, something the British abhorred.

"Had you visited this house before the closing?" Holmes asked, taking out a notebook and pen.

"Yes, I arrived in England three days ago, and I was staying with a friend across the river."

"And who might he be?"

"She. Dame Felicity Devonshire."

Holmes nodded. "Quite."

"She showed me the house and introduced me to Ms. Blackburn, on my first day here."

"And when did you meet Sir Charles for the first time?"

"At dinner that evening."

"Dinner here?"

"No, in Cowes."

"Where in Cowes?"

"At the Royal Yacht Squadron."

"Just the two of you?"

"No, in the company of Dame Felicity. It was at that dinner that I offered to buy this property."

"Having seen it only once?"

57

"I had two very good guides earlier that day."

"Did you come to England specifically to buy the property?"

"Yes, but I didn't know it until after I arrived."

Holmes looked at him sharply. "Explain, please."

"I was in Rome. Dame Felicity called and insisted I come to England, saying she had a surprise for me. The surprise turned out to be this house. I wrote a check for it that evening."

"Then you must be a very wealthy man, Mr. Barrington."

Stone smiled. "You *are* a detective, aren't you?"

Holmes permitted himself a small smile. "Quite. And when did you depart London to return here?"

"About half past ten, from Berkeley Square."

"And you were driving the German sports car?"

"I was."

"Pick that up in London, did you?"

"I did. And another car, as well."

"Didn't see that one."

"Ms. Blackburn had so much luggage it required another car. It should be here early this afternoon."

"That is a calumny," Susan said. She pointed at Stone. "*He* is the one with all the luggage."

"I won't get in the middle of that argument," Holmes said. "Ms. Blackburn, do you believe that Mr. Barrington murdered Sir Richard Curtis?"

Susan thought about it for a moment. "Probably not."

Holmes closed his notebook and stood up. "That's good enough for me," he said, "but Mr. Barrington, don't leave town."

Stone laughed. "I'm flying to New York on Monday morning," he said, "unless you arrest me first."

"I'm sorry," Holmes said, "I made myself sound like Bulldog Drummond there for a moment, didn't I?"

"Just a bit."

"Let's leave it at this: if you think of anything else that might help me with my inquiries, please call." He handed Stone a card. "Is that better?"

"Much," Stone replied.

"Good day, then."

"Good day," Stone said, and the man started for the door, but his journey was interrupted by Sir Charles Bourne entering the room, red-faced.

"Filthy weather!" he nearly shouted.

"Sir Charles," Stone said, "may I present Deputy Inspector Holmes? Not Sherlock." Then he turned to Susan. "Probably not? That was a ringing endorsement of my character."

"Oh, well," she said.

8

Sir Charles pulled a silken cord at one side of the fireplace, then opened a cabinet to reveal a very nice bar. "Must have a brandy and soda after that drive," he said.

Elsie appeared, and Charles ordered lunch, then he sat down by the fire and took a pull on his drink. "Good. Now, what's the mystery in the meadow?" he asked.

"It appears that a neighbor of yours has met an untimely death," Stone said, "and Deputy Inspector Holmes is investigating."

"What neighbor?" Charles asked.

"Sir Richard Curtis," Holmes replied, watching Charles carefully.

"Good God!" Charles said. He took another swig of his drink and set it on a side table. "Why would anyone harm Richard?"

"That is the subject of our investigation," Holmes replied, "that and who."

"You don't know?"

"Not yet. We've interviewed your staff, one

by one, and they all appear to have no involvement."

"I should think not," Charles said.

"Sir Charles, have you just arrived from London?"

"I have."

"When did you leave this house yesterday for London?"

"Late in the day — I wanted to avoid the rush-hour traffic in London, so I timed it to arrive around seven."

"And where did you go?"

"I keep a flat in London. I went there and made myself some dinner."

"Were you alone?"

"I was. I read for a while, then went to bed. I had a meeting at nine this morning with Mr. Barrington."

"Did anyone see you when you arrived at your flat?"

"Not that I'm aware of. I have a semi-detached, half a house. The people next door are away on the Continent, I believe."

"Where did you park your car?"

"In the garage in the house."

"And did you drive to your meeting this morning?"

"No, I legged it. It's only ten minutes on foot. Inspector, I've watched enough tele-vision to know that you are trying to prove either my guilt or my innocence."

"Quite."

"I am innocent of any involvement in Richard's death."

"I'm glad to hear it. How long did you know Sir Richard?"

"Since first form at school. We were neighbors then, too. We were also at Eton together. After that he went to Cambridge, I to Oxford."

"So you grew apart then?"

"Oh, no, we remained friends for our . . . his whole life. Have you a suspect?"

"Not as such."

"But you have some idea."

"Some. I can't discuss it further at this time."

Charles downed the remainder of his drink and made himself another. "Anybody else?" he inquired. Heads were shaken, and he sat down again. "I can't believe it," he said. "Richard was in perfect health, he was supposed to outlive me."

"Are you unwell, Sir Charles?"

"Very much so," Charles replied. "I've got a few months, if I'm unlucky."

"Unlucky?"

"I'd rather fall off the twig before getting sicker," he said.

"I understand."

"I very much doubt it."

"Is Sir Richard married?"

"For more than fifty years. They met at Cambridge. Glynnis is healthy as a horse. I'd better go see her at once," he said, standing. "Have you anything else to ask me?"

"I believe your wife died some years ago."

"That is correct."

"Are you seeing anyone?"

"A woman, you mean? I'm marrying one on Sunday."

Stone was surprised. "Congratulations, Charles."

"Thank you. That's the real reason for the party. It's not my birthday quite yet. Her name is Elizabeth Bowen. She's a solicitor in the village. I thought we'd surprise everybody, then bugger off to Paris for a few days."

"I congratulate you, as well, Sir Charles," Holmes said. "And I have no further questions for you at this time. Perhaps we'll talk again before Monday."

"I have one for you, Inspector. How was Richard killed?"

"With a knife," Holmes replied. "A rather large one, apparently. His head was half cut off."

"Good God," Charles said again, and sadly. "I'd better go and see Glynnis."

"Will you dine with us this evening, Charles?" Stone asked.

"We've plans in the village, Stone, but thank you." He left without anything further said.

"Sounds like someone took him from behind," Stone said to Holmes. "Commando style."

"Quite," Holmes replied. "And we have four former Royal Marines within spitting distance, counting Sir Richard."

"Major Bugg, then."

"Yes, and Sir Charles, and Wilfred Burns."

"Wilfred? Our hermit?"

"Quite. He grew up with Sir Charles and Sir Richard and was at Eton and Oxford. They were all serving senior officers during the Falklands War. Major Bugg was a subaltern in that one — he's a good deal younger than they." Holmes consulted his watch. "Well, if you'll excuse me, I have a corpse to clear off your meadow and a suspect to question." He closed the door behind him.

"I love it," Susan said.

"Love what?"

"Four Royal Marines, one of them dead, the others, suspects. And they all knew how to use a knife, didn't they?"

"You have an evil mind."

"I do, don't I?" She stood up. "I think I'll

65

go have a nap before dinner."

"Tell me," Stone said, "where is the Lilac Room?"

"Never you mind," she said. She kissed him on the cheek and left him alone in the library.

After a moment, Stone went to the desk and jotted off a note to Sir Charles, offering to fly him and Elizabeth Bowen to Paris the Monday after their wedding, and give them use of his home there during their honeymoon. He'd have to refuel between England and the Azores anyway, and the house was just sitting empty. After summoning Elsie and asking her to convey the note to Sir Charles, Stone headed upstairs.

9

Stone went up to the master suite, unpacked his things and arranged them in his dressing room, then he stretched out on his bed for a nap. Before he could close his eyes the phone on the bedside table rang. "Yes?"

"Mr. Barrington, it's Mrs. Whittle. What time would you like dinner?"

"Seven-thirty?"

"Very good. In the library?"

"Yes, thank you." He hung up and fell asleep. It was getting dark when the phone rang again. "Yes?"

"Where and what time are we dining?" Susan asked.

"Let's meet in the library at seven, for drinks."

"And what is the dress?"

"Since it's in the library, I'll wear a necktie."

"That's all the advice I need," she said. "See you in ten minutes." She hung up.

Stone looked at the bedside clock: ten to seven. He bounced out of bed, got into a blazer, gray flannels, and a striped tie, and walked down the stairs to the library, which he found empty, but with a fire alight and the card table set. The remaining half-bottle of the Batard-Montrachet was in an ice bucket beside the table and a bottle of Romanée-Conti La Tache was on the table, open and breathing. He was still trying to calculate the cost of the wine he was drinking that day when Susan swept in, wearing a black cocktail dress and gorgeous jewelry. "Evening, all," she said.

"Evening. Drink?"

"You did such a nice martini at lunch, I'll have that again, please."

Stone mixed it, poured, and set it on a silver tray with his bourbon, then offered it to her. "Someone was kind enough to lay in a stock of Knob Creek," he said.

"The staff are anticipating your wishes," Susan replied. "It's off to a good start, you are."

They sat down on the sofa facing the fire, where a tray of canapés awaited them. "I'm beginning to feel at home already," Stone said, "and it's not even twenty-four hours that I've owned the house."

"When I'm done here you'll feel even

more at home," she said. "It's a specialty of mine, making the owner feel at home in his house."

"May I place an order with you?"

"Of course."

"I like the king-sized mattress on my bed — very comfortable — but I would prefer a pair of extra-long twins that can be electrically adjusted. Also, I haven't been able to find the television set."

"Beds noted — I have a source. On your return from America, they will have been installed, and I'll have fitted sheets for you, too. Do you like the Irish linen sheets?"

"Very much, as long as they're changed or ironed every day."

"I will convey that to Elsie. Mmmm, this is a very fine martini."

"And the TV set?"

"It arises from a piece of antique furniture at the foot of your bed, and its remote control is in the bedside table drawer."

"How long have you been working on this house?"

"About fourteen months," she replied. "Of course, that includes waiting times for almost everything to arrive."

"What have you done here that I can't see?"

"Well, we've reupholstered seventy pieces

of furniture, virtually everything except a dozen or so leather pieces that have worn well with age. We've replaced all the house's main systems — boilers and air-conditioning system — refinished many of the mahogany and walnut pieces of furniture, installed a twenty-four-extension office-quality telephone system, new TV sets and DVRs in every bedroom, and in here, had the Steinway grand completely rebuilt and refurbished."

"I didn't know there was a piano. Where is it?"

"On a truck, on the way down, be here tomorrow. Where would you like it?"

"In this room, I think," he said, pointing. "Over there."

"It shall be done. Do you play?"

"A bit. I played my first gig in twenty years last Saturday night, in Positano."

"Where in Positano? La Sirenuse, perhaps?"

"No, in a private house owned by a very important mafioso. My co-instrumentalists were a guitarist who is a policeman, a bassist who is an officer of the CIA, and a drummer who is the police commissioner of New York City. I also wore a false nose and mustache and pretended to be blind."

She laughed. "That sounds like a fascinating story. Tell it to me, please, all of it."

Stone gave her a fifteen-minute version of the events in Italy.

She couldn't stop laughing. "Your girlfriend must be very grateful to you."

"On the contrary, she punched me in the face at the first opportunity and hasn't spoken to me since."

"Why, the ungrateful bitch! Does she know about the reward you posted for her return?"

"Probably not, and I'm not going to tell her. Anyway, her stepfather has offered to reimburse me, and I have bashfully accepted."

"Is your life always like this?"

"Only occasionally. It's rather sedate, most of the time."

"Tell me about it."

"I have a better idea, I'll show you."

"And how would you accomplish that?"

"I will put you aboard my airplane on Monday morning, fly you to New York, with an overnight stop in the Azores, and you can stay as long as you like."

"That's a tempting thought," she said. "I'll think about it."

"You've had your martini. All you need now is a glass of wine, and you can make a decision."

She held out her glass. "I'll settle for another martini — that should do it."

When the martini was half gone she set down her glass. "You know, I have a couple of clients in New York that I could catch up with. What are the sleeping arrangements at your house?"

"Two large, electrically operated beds, hard by each other."

"Hmmmmm. More thought. I'll give you my answer in the morning."

"I will wait with bated breath," he said.

They finished their dinner, had brandy and coffee, then walked upstairs, paused at the top for a kiss, then went their separate ways.

The following morning, Stone lay naked in bed, sleeping soundly. He turned onto his side and encountered another naked body. He felt it, for identification purposes. "You'd better not be Charles," he said, and got a loud laugh.

She rolled over to face him, and their bodies became entwined. "I accept your gracious invitation to come to New York with you," she said, "pending confirmation of our carnal compatibility."

"I'll get right to work on that," Stone said, kissing her.

10

They made love again. "On a scale of one to ten," he said when they lay panting and spent, "how would you rate our carnal compatibility?"

"Off the charts," she said. "I'm looking forward to New York. If I make a call, I can get a few things sent down from my house in London on one of the trucks."

"Don't forget your passport."

"That is always in my possession. One never knows when one might receive an enticing invitation."

Stone picked up the phone. "What would you like for breakfast?"

"Oh, no you don't," she said, leaping out of bed and getting into a dressing gown. "I'm not giving the staff anything to gossip about. I'll order from the Lilac Room."

"And where is the Lilac Room?"

"Next door." She kissed him and ran out the door.

Stone ordered breakfast, and while he waited for it, found the remote control in the bedside drawer and pressed the On button. A large flat-screen TV rose from the chest at the end of his bed, and the sound came from speakers scattered about the room. He surfed a bit then selected the BBC and watched the morning news.

After breakfast he took the elevator down to the ground floor and tapped on Major Bugg's doorjamb. "Good morning, Major," he said, "may we talk?"

"Of course, Mr. Barrington. Please come in and take a pew." He gestured to a chair across his desk.

"Are you going to preach to me?" Stone asked as he settled into it.

"Not unless that's what you'd like."

"I'd like a rundown on how the place works, if you don't mind."

Bugg took a bound document from a desk drawer and handed it to him. "This is our year-end summary for last year," he said. "We publish one every month, as well. It details all our expenses in detail. There's no income to speak of, except for the surplus milk we sell to the Cadland Dairy across the river."

Stone found a list of staff salaries and read

down it, starting with Bugg, then he found a monthly summary of expenses. "This looks very much in order," he said, "but when I get back to New York I'll have my accountant go over it. I may have questions then. In the meantime, I find the staff underpaid."

"Our salaries are in line with what others in the neighborhood pay."

"Please give them a twenty-five percent raise, yours included, and tell them that it's based on their not gossiping to others about what they're earning."

"That's very generous of you, Mr. Barrington. I'll certainly pass that admonition along to them, though I can't promise they won't brag a bit."

"I think people who are well paid perform better and are more loyal than those who are underpaid."

Bugg nodded. "By the way, the police arrested the brigadier last night and will be charging him with the murder of Sir Richard Curtis."

"Who is the brigadier?" Stone asked.

"I'm sorry, it's our hermit, Wilfred Burns."

"He's a brigadier general?"

"Royal Marines, retired. We all of us here served under him during the Falklands War."

"Ah, that's right, there are four Royal Marines on the property, I had been told."

"Quite right. The brigadier was a colonel and our regimental commander during the war. Sir Charles was a lieutenant colonel, a company commander, and his executive officer, Sir Richard commanded another company. I was a freshly minted subaltern, leading a commando platoon. The war was good for all of us. Colonel Burns became brigadier, and Sir Charles succeeded him as colonel and regimental commander, with Sir Richard as his executive officer. I was promoted to captain and made regimental adjutant, or administrative officer."

"And how did the brigadier become a hermit?"

"A sad story," Bugg said. "He was a confirmed bachelor and something of a swashbuckler with the ladies. Unfortunately, he swashed his buckle once too often with the wife of a brother officer — this after he had made brigadier. He had hoped, with good reason, to rise to commanding general of the Royal Marines, but it was made clear to him that he would never make major general, and he resigned and took his pension. Sir Charles and Sir Richard packed it in soon after, pretty much in protest of his treatment. I stayed on for another fifteen

76

years, and I retired when Sir Charles offered me this job. I live in a cottage on the estate with my wife. We have one son, who is grown, now, and living in London."

"How did the brigadier take his treatment by the Royal Marines?"

"He was devastated. Sir Charles had come into this place, and the brigadier approached him and asked to move onto the property as hermit. Sir Charles built a tiny cottage for him in a patch of woods, and he made do with his pension and by keeping the woods, thinning it and selling firewood from his work. He shaved only twice a year: once in January, for the regimental reunion, and once in August, for the Squadron Ball, at the end of the Cowes Week regatta. He turned out in uniform and was charming and gregarious on both occasions. Otherwise, he lived quietly and rarely spoke to anyone."

"Have you heard what his motive for killing Sir Richard might have been?"

"I have not."

"I'd like you to find him a solicitor, a good one from the county, and have him seen in jail before the day is out. He's going to find the experience depressing, and I want him to know that he's being taken care of. I'd like to speak to the solicitor today, after he's seen the brigadier. By phone will be fine."

"Certainly, I can do that. In fact, I know just the man: Sir Thomas Everly. He'll prepare the defense and he'll know the right barrister for the trial."

"That's fine." Stone handed him his card. "This is my New York address and phone number. My secretary's name is Joan Robertson, and you'll find her very good to deal with. I'll have her call and introduce herself. Joan will make regular deposits into the household account, so you can submit your monthly needs to her and she will move the money."

"Thank you, I'll look forward to speaking with her."

A trim woman in her forties came to the door and knocked.

"Mr. Barrington, this is my assistant and bookkeeper, Miss Edgeware."

Stone rose and shook her hand. "I'm sorry to interrupt," she said, "but there's a call for Mr. Barrington."

"Of course," the major said.

"It's Deputy Chief Inspector Holmes on line one."

Bugg pointed to a phone on a small conference table behind Stone, and he turned and picked it up. "Good morning, Inspector."

"I wish it were so, Mr. Barrington. I am sorry to tell you that your hermit, Brigadier Wilfred Burns, took his own life in the wee hours of the morning."

Stone sucked in a breath. "I'm sorry to hear that, too, Inspector. How did he accomplish that? Was he not under guard?"

"He tore a bedsheet into strips, made a rope, and hanged himself from the bars in a high window. He was under guard, as all our prisoners are, but not under suicide watch, as we had no reason, after speaking with and observing him, to think he was at risk."

"Did he make any statement after his arrest?"

"He declined to speak to us and asked for a solicitor. We would have provided him one today. He also left a note in his cell, confessing to the murder and telling us where to find the weapon, a military knife."

"Did he explain his motive?"

"He did not."

"Do you have any reason to believe that his confession was not credible?"

"None. I was convinced early on that he was our man."

"Thank you, Inspector. I'll see that his remains are collected for burial."

"There will have to be an autopsy, of

course, and that cannot take place before Monday, perhaps Tuesday. I will ring you when the remains are available."

"I'm leaving for New York on Monday morning, so please ring Major Bugg at this number. He will be authorized to make the necessary arrangements."

"I bid you good day, then."

"Good day." Both men hung up.

Stone turned toward Bugg. "The brigadier hanged himself in his cell last night."

"Good God!"

"He left a note, confessing to the killing. Is there a burial ground on the property?"

"St. Mark's Church across the road, just outside our gates. I'll make arrangements with the vicar and the undertaker."

"Thank you. The inspector will phone you early next week, after an autopsy has been performed, to let you know when the body can be collected."

"He was fierce when leading his men in battle," Bugg said, "and was highly decorated, but I cannot imagine him killing anyone, particularly Sir Richard, of whom he was fond."

"I'll leave it to you to inform the next of kin and see that all expenses are met."

"I already know there is no next of kin. The staff here were his family."

"I'm sorry I won't be here for the services," Stone said. "I'll speak to you on Monday morning before I leave. Will you inform Sir Charles of these events?"

"Of course."

Stone left Bugg's office and went to find Susan.

11

Stone called Susan on her cell phone.

"Hello?"

"Where are you?"

"In the cellar, in the boiler room. Come have a look."

Stone found the stairs down and shouted her name until she answered. He found her in a clean, well-lit room with gleaming machinery humming away.

"I wanted you to see this," she said. "It's emblematic of the way Sir Charles kept the house. And I expect you'd like to see the wine cellar, as well."

"Of course." He followed her down a hallway, and she opened the door with a key and switched on the lights. "I had this constructed, then inventoried the bottles and arranged them by type and vintage." Stone looked around and reckoned there must be forty or more cases of wine. He looked at some of the labels and found they had been laid down years before.

"Sir Charles has already selected his two dozen bottles and removed them," she said. "Where have you been this morning?"

"Going over things with Major Bugg," Stone replied. "He told me that the brigadier had been arrested last night."

"Who is the brigadier?"

Stone told her the whole story, including the phone call from the inspector.

"That's awful," she said. "Is this going to affect our departure date?"

"Not in the least. I've done all I can do, and there's no reason for us to hang about another week for the funeral. I never even spoke to the man."

"Good. My men in the vans called a few minutes ago. They should be here any minute, so I'll have to go upstairs and place the furniture and the pictures."

They walked upstairs together. "What rooms will be used for the party?"

"The drawing room, the dining room, and the library. Everything for all three rooms will be in the vans. Actually, I'm much closer to being finished than Sir Charles realizes. From today, it's mostly cleaning and polishing. My assistant will be in charge while I'm gone. I'll plan to stay in New York for a week or so, and when I get back I'll do a walk-around and make lists of things that are imperfect. In a couple of weeks your house will be done. When will you see it again?"

"Late spring, I should think."

"A good idea to wait for spring weather. Most Americans can't handle our winters."

"I'm not one of them. I love this country the year 'round. It's beautiful when it rains, though not necessarily on the motorway in a deluge."

"That's more than a lot of Englishmen would say."

"If you know a good restaurant, I'll take you out for dinner."

"I'm happy to dine in. I'll be tired by the time everything is in place. I have a lot of pictures to hang, too."

"Can I help?"

"Certainly not, you'd just be in the way." She kissed him. "Now go take a nap, or something."

Stone went back to the master suite, arranged himself in a comfortable armchair with his feet up, and called Dino.

"Where the hell have you been?" Dino demanded. "I've heard all sorts of crazy rumors about you buying a country estate in England."

"They're all true," Stone said, "and I can't

84

wait to show you the place. It's just terrific."

"Look, I know you've always imagined yourself as an English gentleman, but now you've gone — what do they say over there?"

"Around the bend," Stone replied, "and loving it. I'm flying home Monday morning and bringing a delightful woman who is the designer on the renovation of the house. Let's have dinner Wednesday night."

"I guess it's just as well you managed to get rid of the last one so quickly."

"I haven't heard a word from her, so I guess she's still angry."

"I tried to reason with her on the flight home from Rome, to no avail. When I told her about the reward you and Marcel posted, it made her even madder. She said she was going to make Arthur repay you."

"Arthur has already offered, and I accepted before he could change his mind. That's why I can afford this house — that and if I sell the Washington, Connecticut, place to Bill Eggers."

"Take pictures of the house," Dino said. "Viv will kill us both if you don't. She's already planning a visit, but I haven't had time yet to explain to the mayor what I was doing in Rome for ten days. I've been avoiding seeing or speaking to him."

"That sounds like a good policy."

"Always. Now go take pictures."

Stone did so, with his iPhone, outside and in.

12

Stone was dressing for Sunday night's event when he heard voices and car doors slamming at the front of the house. He peered through the curtains and saw people getting out of Jaguars and Range Rovers, dressed to the nines. They were on time, and he was glad he was not the evening's host.

Someone rapped on his bedroom door, and he admitted Susan, in a tight red dress and a spectacular necklace.

"I'm not expected to be ready on time, am I," he asked, "not being the host?"

"I suppose not. May I have a drink?"

"I'll have to ring downstairs for it, and I think they must be pretty busy."

"You haven't explored your suite, have you?" She walked to a corner of the room and tugged on what looked like a bell cord for summoning servants. Two panels in the wall slid silently open, revealing a small wet bar.

"You've anticipated my every need," Stone said, mixing her a martini. "Even an ice machine."

"I have," she replied.

He poured himself a Knob Creek. "You look good enough to molest," he said, "if it weren't for that dress."

"It comes off quite easily," she said, "but you can't muss my makeup. It goes back on very slowly. Can you restrain yourself until a bit later, when we don't have guests to greet?"

"Oh, I suppose," he said.

"May I tie your bow tie?"

"If it would please you."

She buttoned his collar, took hold of both ends of the tie, made a little motion, and it was tied. He checked the mirror. "How did you do that? It takes me three times longer to get it right, and you've done it perfectly the first time."

"Innate skill," she replied, "and a little practice."

They tapped glasses and drank.

"Mmmm," she said, "you do make a good martini, and it's good to have a head start on the others. I wouldn't want to go downstairs entirely sober."

"Then you shan't," Stone said. "What do you have left to do to this room?"

"Hanging of the curtains — these are temporary — and pictures — that's about it. Oh, I picked up a very nice rug for it, too."

More car doors were slamming outside, and Stone slipped into his jacket, tucked a white satin pocket square into his breast pocket and a jotter pad and his pen into an inside one. "There. Let's go downstairs and face them." They both tossed off the rest of their drinks and walked out the door and downstairs into the hall, where Sir Charles and Elizabeth Bowen were greeting their guests.

"Stone, come stand with us," Charles said, "and meet your new neighbors, and Susan, you come and take compliments. Everything in the house looks splendid."

They joined the couple and Stone began to meet his neighbors. More than half of them, he noted, were wearing Squadron mess kits, and he was introduced to several of them as officers in the club, one of them the commodore. Each of them took a few minutes to talk with him and compliment Susan on the house. When the arrivals trickled to a stop they took a stroll around the room, meeting others.

"You've really done a wonderful job," Stone said. "This is the first time I've seen completed rooms."

"Thank you, kind sir. Come this way." She led him into the hall and showed him his Constable, which he liked very much, then into the library, where a pianist was playing, and he came face-to-face with his other new art acquisition. "This is your new Turner," she said. "It's called *Storm over Cowes.*"

Stone was amazed. The castle was in the foreground, and a storm raged at sunset over the village. Boats were in disarray, and people ran for shelter. "I've never seen such a sky," he said.

"If you spend a few summers in Cowes, you will one day, it's guaranteed."

Charles came and stood next to them. "I was a fool to sell it," he said.

"Well," Stone said, "I'm not giving it back."

Charles clapped his hands, and the pianist stopped his tune and played a fanfare. "My Lords and Ladies, ladies and gentlemen," he called out, "please come in from the hall and gather in the library." People came in and filled the large room.

Charles took Elizabeth's hand and moved her before the fireplace, where a man stood, holding a book.

"I know this may come as a shock," Sir Charles said. "It certainly shocked me, but

Elizabeth Bowen has condescended to become my wife."

Applause and delighted laughs broke out. "Stone, will you and Susan stand up for us?"

"Of course," Stone said, and escorted Susan to the fireplace. It was over very quickly: the magistrate asked the right questions and got the right answers, and he pronounced them man and wife. The magistrate gave the bride and groom and their witnesses the certificate to sign, then Charles handed it to Major Bugg. "Put that in the safe," he said. "Now, all of you, a buffet is being served in the dining room, and you must be starved."

The guests got their food and arrayed themselves around the drawing room and the library, and a good time was had by all.

Toward the end of the evening Stone and Susan were nestled on the big sofa in the library, before the fireplace. The last of the party guests finally left the room.

"Finally," Susan said, sipping her brandy.

Then the door opened and someone came in. Stone and Susan scrunched down so as not to be seen.

"Thank you for inviting my sister and me," a man said.

"I thought it the decent thing to do,"

Charles replied.

"I've wanted to talk to you for a long time, and given how little time you've got left, according to my sources, I want to know about my father and how this horrible mess came about."

"It's quite simple," Charles said: "Our marriage had hardly begun when your mother began sleeping with a man I thought was a very good friend of mine. I became suspicious when the sex tapered off until nothing, then on two occasions she seduced me, much to my surprise, and a month or so after each occasion, she turned up pregnant, first with you, then with your sister. I still didn't twig until that time you cut your arm when we were out sailing. Do you remember?"

"I remember — it was a horrible experience."

"All the more so for me. We got a tourniquet on you, then docked and took you to the casualty ward at the hospital, where the doctor informed me that you needed an immediate transfusion but that your blood group was a rare one. There were half a dozen of us there, but only one had the correct blood group. Your mother had arrived, and she didn't have the correct group, either, but you were transfused and your life saved. You and your sister had the same blood group, and neither your mother nor I had it, but this one chap, my friend, did."

"I've asked her many times who our father was, because it was so obvious that you were not. Who is he?"

"He's dead these many years, and if your mother didn't want you to know, I certainly don't. Now, there's an end to it. By the way, if you haven't already heard, I've sold the house and land to an American gentleman, along with the contents and the livestock, so you and your sister may put any thought of inheriting out of your minds."

"It's like you to leave us with nothing," the younger man said.

"Your mother took very good care of you both in her will, so I feel no such obligation. Now, I bid you good night and farewell. We shan't be speaking again."

The door opened again and slammed behind them.

"My goodness," Susan said.

"Your goodness, indeed. I'm sorry we heard that — it was more than I wanted to know."

"Then you're a great deal less curious than I."

They went upstairs, and he did what she had invited him to do earlier. When they were sated with each other Susan asked, "What is the plan for tomorrow?"

"We leave the house at nine AM and make the short trip to Southampton International Airport. Our flight planning has already been done and filed by a service in New York, so we only have to stow our luggage, hop in, and fly. We'll be in Paris in about forty minutes, where we will refuel and take off for Horta, in the Azores, where we will refuel again and perhaps stay the night. If the winds are more unfavorable than forecast, we'll land at Santa Maria, which is closer. I had thought we'd overnight in Horta, but what with the time difference and the forecast winds, we can continue to St. John's, in Newfoundland, where we refuel yet again, then continue to Teterboro, New Jersey, which is just across the Hudson from New York City. None of our legs is more than about three hours, and we should be at my house in the late afternoon, tired and sleepy. We'll have a good dinner at home, then I will ravish you, and we will sleep like puppies. How does that sound for a day?"

"It sounds just perfect," she said.

13

Stone was barely awake at dawn, when Susan crept out of bed and went to the Lilac Room to order her breakfast. He had his eggs alone, then showered, shaved, dressed, and closed his suitcases. He and Susan met Sir Charles and Lady Bourne, as arranged, at the car, and Stan came with them to the airport to drive the car home.

Their flight to Le Bourget was short and uneventful, and they said goodbye there.

"Thank you very much for the offer of your house," Charles said. "It is very kind of you."

"Thank you for a very fine property and the opportunity to meet so many of your friends last evening," Stone said.

Their car arrived, and the driver took their luggage. Stone gave Charles the address of the house, and they said goodbye, knowing that they probably would not meet again.

Then, with the airplane refueled, they took

off in clear skies for Horta, in the Azores. Half an hour later they were at flight level 410 — forty-one thousand feet — with a true airspeed of 430 knots and a ground speed of 410. Stone pointed to a dotted circle on the center screen of the panel. "This is the range ring," he said to Susan. "It shows us how far we can fly and still have forty-five minutes of fuel left. As you can see, Horta is well within our range."

"Wonderful. Is it possible to make calls on my cell from the airplane?"

"No, but we have a satellite phone."

"May I make some business calls?"

"Of course. Why don't you make yourself comfortable in the right rear seat. A table is built into the wall — pull up and out. The phone is across the aisle, built into the bulkhead. It's just as if you were calling from another country."

"I know all about that," she said, taking off her seat belt.

Five minutes later he looked back and saw her talking on the phone and making notes on a pad resting on the foldout table.

He flew on, checking the range ring every few minutes, happy that his new airplane had the range to fly this route, rather than going north through Iceland, where there was the constant threat of bad weather outside the summer months.

They refueled at Horta, then continued on to St. John's and, after refueling, to Teterboro, New Jersey, where the airplane was based at Jet Aviation. They were met by U.S. Customs and cleared, then their luggage was taken on a cart to the front door of the FBO, where Stone's factotum, Fred Flicker, awaited them with the car. Forty minutes later they were at home, then they got a good night's sleep.

The following morning, Stone gave Susan a tour of the house, pointing out his mother's paintings, then took her down to his office and introduced her to Joan, who had piled his mail and messages on his desk.

"I'd like to unpack, now," Susan said, "and you seem to have enough to keep you busy here."

"Phone down to the kitchen, and Helene will bring you some lunch, then meet me in my study for drinks at six," he said, "and we'll have dinner there." She left, and Stone called Dino.

"You're still alive?" Dino asked.

"You always ask me that, as if you expect a different outcome."

"One of these days," Dino said. "I hope your flight was uneventful."

"We had a little weather at St. John's and

had to fly the instrument approach, but the rest was severe clear."

"We still on for dinner tomorrow night?"

"We are: seven-thirty at Patroon?"

"See you then."

Stone hung up and tackled his mail. Additional copies of the closing documents on the house had been sent from the London office, and he instructed Joan: "File these under Windward Hall." There was a note from Arthur Steele, confirming his wish to pay the reward Stone had offered for the rescue of his stepdaughter, Hedy. "File this under 'Thank God,' " he told Joan.

Shortly, Joan announced that Bill Eggers was on line one.

"Hello, Bill."

"Did you have a good flight?"

"An excellent one. Did you like the house?"

"How soon can you get out?"

"As soon as I've accepted your offer."

Bill made him one.

"Done. You can move in tomorrow."

"We've already moved in," Bill said. "I can't get the wife to go back to the city."

"Just pack up my clothes — there aren't many — and drop them off here when you get back. I'll get Herb Fisher to close the sale."

"Nice doing business with you."

"Tell me that when you get your first heating bill," Stone replied. He hung up and went back to work.

They met in his study, where Fred had set a table before the fireplace, and he made her a martini and himself a bourbon.

"The house is lovely," Susan said.

"Tell me what you would do to improve the place."

"It's perfect — I can't think of a thing. Who was your designer?"

"I was, for better or worse. Of course, it didn't get done overnight. I had years to get it right."

"That's always the best way. One of the reasons I've succeeded in my work is that I work hard to make it look as though someone has always lived there."

"Tell me, what did Sir Charles's renovation of Windward Hall come to?"

"My budget was two million pounds, but he kept adding things, so the final figure will be closer to three million."

"God, I'm glad I didn't have to do that."

"You are a very fortunate buyer, and my guess is that you are, in general, a lucky man."

"Sometimes I think so, sometimes not."

"Tell me, who are these people we're dining with tomorrow evening?"

"Dino Bacchetti and his wife, Vivian. Dino and I were partners when I was on the NYPD. Now he's the police commissioner, which is the top job there. Viv was a detective who worked for him. She retired from the department to avoid the nepotism problem, and joined Strategic Services, a very large security company, where she has done well and risen in the ranks. She now runs their home office in New York and supervises international."

"They're going to think me very dull," she said.

"Not a bit of it. You'll be fast friends."

"I hope so."

14

When Stone came downstairs to go to work the following morning, there was a strange man sitting in the chair opposite his desk who stood up and offered his hand.

"Hello, Stone," he said. "Billy Barnett."

It took Stone a second to flip through the name change and Teddy Fay's incredible facility with anonymity. "Hello, Billy," he said. "What a nice surprise to see you." His mind raced through the possible reasons for "Billy," as he now was, to leave Los Angeles and come to New York. Stone poured him some coffee and bade him sit down. "What brings you to New York?" Something must be amiss with Peter, Stone's son, he thought; he was not far wrong.

"I'm worried about Peter and Ben," Billy said. Ben was Peter's partner in the film business and he was also Dino's son.

"What's wrong?" Stone asked.

"Problems have arisen that are connected

101

to Peter's new film, *Hell's Bells.*"

"This is the one about a violent fundamentalist sect operating out of some corner of L.A.?"

"Correct. His script was based on snippets of news stories he'd seen over the past couple of years, and he was intrigued by the idea of such a backward group living in a major American city. He invented the greater part of it, but the problem, it seems, is that what he invented is too close to the truth — or, at least, these people have come to believe it is."

"Has he received threats?"

"Insinuations, mainly. They're too smart to make direct threats. In the past, when they've brought pressure to bear on people they believe to be a danger to them, they've always managed to seem to be freshly scrubbed and all-American when the police showed up at their door, and they've given television interviews that reinforce that appearance."

"What are they called?"

"The Chosen Few," Billy said. "They're led by a man named Don Beverly Calhoun, or Dr. Don."

"That is a vaguely familiar name," Stone said. "Where have I heard it?"

"Dr. Don was the pastor of a church in

Atlanta that grew into the sort of organization that congregated in basketball stadiums, instead of a church. He first got noticed when he opposed former president Will Lee in his first run for the Senate, more than twenty-five years ago. The whole thing crumbled when a mixture of financial, sexual, and political scandals converged, and Dr. Don experienced the modern media equivalent of being tarred, feathered, and ridden out of town on a rail. He disappeared for a while, then finally reappeared in New Orleans, then Albuquerque, only to be run out of town again, and, finally, in L.A. about eight years ago. According to one article I read, he hung on to his mailing lists from his old church, particularly one containing the names of his most rabid parishioners, a few dozen of whom followed him wherever he went. The author of the magazine piece was killed in a car crash on the freeway that was very suspicious, but the police never made an arrest."

"I've been out of the country for the past three weeks," Stone said, "and I haven't had a chance to call Peter since I got home Monday night. When does his film open?"

"This weekend, on twelve hundred screens. Centurion Studios has been spooked by the whole thing, and they've cut the number of screens by a thousand and the promotion budget in half, hoping that it will open quietly, then grow slowly on word of mouth."

"Is Peter going to be in L.A. for the opening?"

"We all flew in last night on the Centurion jet — Peter, Ben, and their girlfriends and my wife."

"Is there a formal premiere?"

"No, that was going to happen in L.A. but Centurion canceled it, and they haven't scheduled any New York publicity for Peter, either."

"Where are they staying?"

"At the Carlyle."

"Why didn't they stay here?"

"Peter didn't really want you to know about all this, and anyway, Centurion is paying, so why not?"

"I guess the room service is better at the Carlyle."

"I expect so."

Stone reached for the phone.

"Please, don't call Peter," Billy said.

"Why not?"

"Because then he'll know that I told you about this, and he already thinks I'm an alarmist. He'll call you, don't worry."

"Do you have some plan for dealing with

this, Billy?"

"If it were up to me, I'd put a bullet in the head of Dr. Don some dark night, but as it is, I think we're going to have to wait for developments, then fight back the best way we can. Peter doesn't even want to think about it, so I've pretty much shut up."

"Do you think these people pose an immediate threat to Peter and Ben?"

"I think they're capable of anything," Billy replied, "but I can't predict what."

"I think, perhaps, we should get the kids out of the country."

"I've suggested that, but Peter is not in a mood to run from the situation."

"Maybe what he needs," Stone said, "is a situation to run to."

15

Peter finally called after lunch. "Hi, Dad."

"Hi, there, kiddo. I was about to call you. How are things in L.A.?"

"I'm in New York, for a screening — so are Ben and Billy and theirs. The studio put us at the Carlyle, so we didn't trouble you."

"I got in from England Monday night."

"What were you doing in England?"

"I was finding you a country estate location for a movie."

"Well, that's interesting, I'm working on something I'd like to shoot in a place like that. Where is it?"

"On the Beaulieu River" — Stone spelled it for him — "in the south of England, near the Solent. Do you know where that is?"

"I've got a map right here, hang on." There was a rustling of paper.

"Right next to Southampton Water."

"Got it, and I see the Solent and the Isle of Wight. Tell me about it."

"As long as you're this far east, why don't you just go over there and look at it? Take a vacation."

"Hattie would like to hear that word from me."

"There's nothing to stop you working while you're there. If you're going to write about England, why not write *in* England?"

"That's not the worst idea you've ever had, Dad. How did you learn about this place?"

"A friend told me about it. If you want to go right after your screening, I'll see if Mike Freeman has a jet going that way. Strategic Services is always back and forth across the Atlantic."

"You don't want to fly us yourself?"

"I just got back. Tell you what, if you'll stay for a while, I'll join you in a couple of weeks, after I've had time to catch up here."

"Where should we stay while we're there? Do you know a good hotel nearby?"

"There's a very nice house on the property, and you'd be comfortable there. There's a staff to take care of you."

"Who owns it?"

"You, eventually."

"Don't tell me you've bought another house!"

"It's all right, I sold one, too. Let's have

dinner tomorrow night, and I'll show you some pictures."

"Okay. And there's a screening of *Hell's Bells* on Friday night we'd all like you to attend. Ben's asking Dino and Viv."

"Wonderful. I'll check with Mike about getting you across the pond."

"Where will we go tomorrow night?"

"Do you still like the Four Seasons?"

"Sure I do, I've missed it."

"Eight o'clock there."

"You're on."

"See you then." They hung up, and Stone called Mike Freeman.

"Welcome home. I hear the new house is beautiful."

"It certainly is. When will you come to visit?"

"Maybe sooner than you think."

"Listen, Peter and Ben and their young women want to go over there this weekend. Do you have an airplane headed that way?"

"I expect so. When do they want to go?"

"Saturday or Sunday?"

"I'll do a little juggling with my people. They'll have to share the airplane, though. How many of them?"

"Six, and there's a seven-thousand-foot runway on the property with a GPS approach. You can drop them there, and I'll arrange for customs and immigration to meet them."

"I'll confirm later today."

"Great, Mike, and thanks."

Joan buzzed him.

"Yes?"

"There's somebody called Deputy Chief Inspector Holmes on line two. He's been holding."

"Got it." Stone punched the button. "Hello, Inspector, sorry to keep you waiting."

"Quite all right," Holmes said. "I've something of a problem, and I hope you can help."

"Certainly, if I can."

"I wish to speak to Sir Charles Bourne, and I can't locate him. Major Bugg says he's out of the country, but he doesn't know where. Do you know?"

"The man's on his honeymoon, Inspector, leave him alone."

"I don't want you to think me unromantic, Mr. Barrington, but I wish to speak with him now."

"Then I suppose you'll just have to wait until he comes home. He won't be hard to find."

"Then you don't know where he is?"

"I'm afraid I can't help, Inspector."

"I've some reason to think he might be in France."

"I can't deny that."

"You know, the French police have a very good system of tracking hotel guests. I could phone them and know in an hour or two what hotel he's staying in."

"What a good idea. Why don't you do that?"

"Thank you, I will." He hung up, miffed.

Stone called his Paris house and got Marie, the housekeeper, on the phone, and she put Sir Charles on. "Hello there, Stone. What a wonderful house! We're enjoying ourselves immensely."

"I'm very glad to hear it," Stone said. "I thought you should know that I've had a call from Deputy Chief Inspector Holmes, inquiring of your whereabouts. He seems anxious to talk with you."

"Well, bugger him," Charles said. "Doesn't the man know I'm on my honeymoon?"

"I mentioned that to him, but he was persistent. He's having the French police find out what hotel you're staying in."

Charles laughed heartily. "He won't have much luck there, will he?"

"You might give him a ring when you get home, Charles."

"Oh, all right, I will. In the meantime, I

have a lot more honeymooning to do."

Stone hung up, and Joan buzzed again. "Mike Freeman on one."

"Mike?"

"How about Friday evening, late — say eleven o'clock? That will put them there early Saturday morning."

"I think that might work out very well," Stone said. "They're going to a movie earlier."

"No later than midnight, though, and you'll arrange customs at your airfield?"

"I will." Stone gave him the identifier for the field. "And thank you, Mike. Once again, I owe you." Stone hung up and called Peter on his cell. "I've got you a free ride across the pond, departing Teterboro at eleven PM Friday. Is that good for you?"

"It's perfect, thanks."

"You'll be landing on the estate, and I'll have you met."

"There'll be six of us. Billy and his wife are coming, too."

"Oh, good. See you tomorrow evening." He hung up, feeling he had done a good day's work.

16

Stone and Susan Blackburn arrived at Patroon to find Dino and Viv already there. He made the introductions.

"And what brings you to New York, Susan?" Viv asked.

"Stone made me an offer I couldn't refuse. I also have a few clients here, and I thought I'd see if I could drum up some business."

"We're delighted to meet you."

"And I'm delighted to be here."

"Has Ben called you?" Stone asked Dino.

"This afternoon," Dino replied. "I understand we're all having dinner tomorrow evening, and we have a screening on Friday."

"That's right, and they're all flying to England Friday night, after the screening."

"How did you talk Peter into that?"

"I told him I had a setting for a film for him, and he told me he was already working on one. Mike Freeman is putting him

on one of Strategic Service's airplanes."
They ordered drinks, and Stone told them
about the visit from Billy Barnett. "It
seemed like a good idea to get them out of
the country for a while."

"How long a while?"

"At least a couple of weeks. I told them
I'd join them then." He turned to Susan.
"If you can stand New York and me for that
long, I'll fly you back."

"I can stand you both," she said. "I'll talk
with my office and see if I can decorate
houses on the phone for that long."

"Are the guest rooms in the house fit for
occupancy?"

"I'll see that they are, and I've already
ordered your electric beds. They'll be there
for you when you return."

"Dino, can you get away again?"

"Absolutely not, but Viv can go, if she
likes."

"I'll see if I can arrange some business to
require my presence," Viv said. "The hell
with Dino."

"I finally had the unavoidable chat with
the mayor," Dino said. "Some pointed questions were asked about the necessity of being in Rome."

"And I'm sure you were ready with the
answers," Stone said.

"He'd already heard most of it, and he took it well. Anyway, he hasn't fired me yet."

They ordered dinner.

"I've heard some things about this Dr. Don," Dino said. "He's made it onto a couple of watch lists."

"Do you think he's dangerous?" Stone asked.

"Well, one magazine reporter is dead — his car blew up on the L.A. freeway shortly after his article on this cult appeared."

"Is that what they are? A cult?"

"They're the fanatical followers of a charismatic religious figure. What else would you call them?"

"You have a point."

"Peter and Ben's movie is opening in twelve hundred theaters," Dino pointed out. "Nobody can cover all of them."

"I'm glad you're getting the kids out of the country," Viv said.

After dinner, the ladies excused themselves.

"I need to talk to you about Billy Barnett," Dino said.

"Okay."

"I've done some checking on his background, and although I can't prove it yet, I think he might very well be Teddy Fay. And if I get to the point where I can prove it,

I'm going to have to do something about it. Fay is a wanted man."

"Not anymore," Stone said.

"What are you talking about?"

"He's not wanted anymore. Run the name through your system and see what you come up with."

Dino took out his iPhone, entered an app, and tapped in the name. "Zilch," he said. "What's going on?"

"I can tell you only if it stops here."

"All right."

"I asked Will Lee to give him a presidential pardon when he was on his way out of office. It was issued sealed, for reasons of national security, and his name was scrubbed from every law enforcement and national security database. Nobody can touch him now."

"That's the craziest thing I ever heard," Dino said.

"It's crazy, until you consider that he saved the lives of my son and yours in L.A. You and I both owe him."

Dino shrugged. "I guess we do. You're sure about the pardon and the databases?"

"You want to try a few more before the girls come back?"

"No, I'll take your word for it."

"You'll get used to the idea, Dino. I have."

115

"I expect I will."

The following morning after making love and having breakfast, Susan disappeared into her dressing room for a few minutes, then came back. "Okay, I can stay on for a while. I'll fly back with you and Viv a week from Saturday, but I absolutely must be in London on the following Monday morning for a meeting with an important prospect."

"Wonderful. We're having dinner tonight with the kids at the Four Seasons, and Friday we're going to a screening of Peter and Ben's new movie. They're off to England after the movie, and we'll fly a week later. It's a shorter flight going back, because of the winds. We might be able to make it nonstop from St. John's."

"Wonderful. I can do some things for one of my clients while I'm here, then have the fabrics shipped from London. I have a source here that can do the installations."

"Do you have other international clients?"

"I do, but I try to keep the number down. The travel gets wearing. There's something in the works that may decrease my workload, though."

"What's that?"

"I have a software group in London that is working on a package that will allow me to send an assistant to a site to photograph the rooms, then I can go online and select from a host of wallpaper and paint colors and combinations and show the client what his room will look like — I can even insert furniture and fabrics into the picture. At least that's the intended outcome. It's an expensive project, because it's being done exclusively for me. When it's perfected, I can license it to other designers with their own sets of fabrics, et cetera, and make money on the investment."

"That's a very smart move," Stone said.

"I've been designing fabrics, rugs, and wallpaper for years, so I have hundreds that are exclusive to me, but I can also draw on other sources, if necessary."

"How big a staff do you have?"

"About thirty, including the new upholstery firm I bought last year. That allows me to do projects much more quickly, instead of waiting in line at other firms. Charles's account was what allowed me to make that investment. Now that we've finished his furniture, we have to get more into the pipeline to keep our people busy."

"Who does your business planning?"

"I do."

"My firm has a substantial London office that can help you with that — everything from real estate acquisitions to financing. You should be planning years ahead and copyrighting your designs, too, if you haven't already."

"I've been meaning to do that for a long time, I just haven't gotten around to it."

"You need a business structure that will allow you to delegate more authority."

"I have a wonderful assistant who's doing a lot of the work now."

"Maybe you need three or four assistants who can do that, then you can sit at your computer anywhere in the world and look at their suggestions, then make final decisions on what to propose to clients."

"Perhaps I should meet with your firm when I get back to London?"

"I'll set that up, if you like."

"I would like that very much."

Stone went down to his office and called Bill Eggers. "I think I have a new client for you in London," he said.

"You're just looking for excuses to use your new house," Eggers said.

"There is that, but what we're talking about is one of Britain's very best interior designers, named Susan Blackburn, who could expand her operation worldwide, but she needs solid business planning, financing, copyright work, and everything else a company needs for expansion. She'll be back in London a week from Monday. Perhaps you could ask Julian Whately to put together a team to evaluate her needs, then draw up a business plan."

"You talked me into it," Eggers said. "Whately is due here next week, anyway. We're reevaluating our own business needs in London, including some hiring and new offices."

"Maybe you'd like to meet with her before they both go back to London."

"She's here? I should have known. Sure, let's set that up. By the way, Herb Fisher is going to be ready for us to close on the Connecticut house by the end of the week. I hope nothing goes wrong — the wife is already looking for a designer."

"Maybe she'd like to have Susan take a look at the house while she's in town."

"I expect she would."

"Then I'll set that up, too."

17

That evening they met at the Four Seasons for dinner. Stone chose the menu, and they dined very well indeed. Afterward Billy Barnett took Stone aside.

"I don't know how you managed to get the boys out of the country so quickly, but I'm glad you did."

"Let's just say that their interests and mine coincided. Have them get packed before the screening, so that they can leave the theater and go straight to Teterboro for the flight. You'll be landing on my property and clearing customs there, too. There will be some Strategic Services people on board, as well, who will be continuing on to London with ground transportation. The airplane will continue on to Paris and overnight there, then fly some other Strategic Services people back to New York."

"Sounds like a large airplane."

"It's a Gulfstream 650."

"How long is your landing strip?"

"Seven thousand feet. It was an RAF base during World War Two."

"That should handle just about anything."

"Have you heard anything more about the Chosen Few?"

"I found out how they're financing themselves. Dr. Don has written a series of books based on conspiracy theories about government encroachment on individual rights."

"Why have I not seen them advertised?"

"Because they're sold only on the Chosen Few website. He gets thirty to forty bucks a book and sells tens of thousands around the country. They make documentary films of the same nature, too, and sell them on DVDs. Dr. Don is bringing in millions a year, and he doesn't have a lot of overhead. There's no church, they rent venues for large meetings, and he only has enough staff to count the money. There are rumors that he has a large vault in his house and keeps most of the cash there."

"Surely the FBI is looking at this guy."

"Almost certainly, but they've never charged him with anything."

"There must have been an investigation of the magazine writer's death."

"By the LAPD, but no charges were ever brought for lack of evidence."

■ ■ ■ ■

The Friday-night screening was a huge success. The invited audience gave it a standing ovation, and Peter and Ben took a bow. Stone hustled them to their cars as quickly as he could. He hugged Peter and Ben. "Have a good flight and call me after you're at the house. The staff will meet you at the airplane and take good care of you. You'll go through customs and immigration at the property."

The boys and their girlfriends and the Barnetts were driven away.

Stone's and Dino's cars were waiting. "Dino," Stone said, "you know the director of the FBI, don't you?"

"I do."

"Why don't you give him a call and see if you can find out what, if anything, they have on Dr. Don and his Chosen Few?"

"I'll call him at home this weekend," Dino said. "I don't want to make an official inquiry."

"Okay. You sure you don't want to go to England next weekend?"

"I'd love to, I really would, but I'm going to have the press on my ass if I keep trying to keep up with you."

"I'm glad Viv can go."

"So am I — she can use some time off."

Stone and Susan continued home. Upstairs, he turned on CNN, having missed the regular evening news.

"A new film opened at twelve hundred theaters across the nation tonight called *Hell's Bells*. Audiences at two of them got more than they had bargained for. There were explosions at theaters in Santa Monica, California, and Coeur d'Alene, Idaho, shortly after the film began. Police in both cities said there were no serious casualties, that the explosions had been caused by the stun grenades police use to storm crime scenes. One Idaho woman was taken to a hospital for cuts and bruises and is being kept overnight for observation. Others at both theaters were treated on-site by EMTs and released."

"Oh, God," Stone said, "it's started." He switched on his iPhone, went to a flight-tracking app, and entered the tail number of the Strategic Services G650. The airplane was halfway to Newfoundland. "I'm glad they're on their way."

The phone rang, and Stone picked it up. "Hello?"

"Hi, Dad."

"Peter? I just checked on your flight — you're halfway to Newfoundland."

"Right, I see that on the flight progress screen. This is some airplane."

"It certainly is."

"We also get CNN. Have you heard what happened at two of our theaters?"

"I just saw it. That's terrible news."

"I'm glad no one was seriously hurt."

"So am I."

"Ben thinks the publicity will help us, rather than hurt us."

"I suppose it could. I'm glad you're not here to get hounded by the media. You'd be wise to keep your destination quiet and let Centurion's PR people handle the press response."

"You don't think I should issue a statement?"

"No, I don't. Just enjoy yourself."

"I'm sure we will. I liked Susan. I hope you'll see a lot more of her."

"I think you can count on that."

"Good night, then."

"Get some sleep and arrive rested." Stone hung up.

18

Stone woke to find an outstanding review of *Hell's Bells* in the *New York Times.* He checked his watch: it was midday in England, and Peter hadn't called yet. He was relieved when the phone rang.

"Hello?"

"Hi, Dad. We made it in good order. Is this too early to call?"

"It's perfect. Want to hear something nice?"

"Sure."

Stone read him a few paragraphs of the review. "I'll fax you the whole thing when I get downstairs."

"Thanks, it's too early to hear from L.A., and it's Saturday. I'll check with them later. Dad, this house is the most beautiful thing I've ever seen, and it's in perfect condition."

"That's because it's just gone through a year-long renovation, top to bottom, all Susan's work."

"She's an incredible designer."

"Does it work for your idea for a film?"

"It certainly does."

"Is it a period piece?"

"Between the world wars. The phones and the TVs are all we'd have to change."

"The TVs are concealed at the press of a button, but you're right about the phones."

"Do you think Susan would like to be our production designer?"

"I'll ask her. By the way, the previous owner, Sir Charles Bourne, is still living on the place, in the largest of the cottages. He's in Paris on his honeymoon, but he should be back soon. I've let him know that you're there, so when you see him introduce yourselves. Also, there are horses, if you feel like riding. Just tell the butler, Geoffrey, and he'll speak to the stable hands."

"I think we're going to be very happy here."

"Well, get to it, then, and give me a call if you have any questions, or see Major Bugg, who runs the place from his basement office. I've got two cars there, too. Use them." Stone hung up and Susan brought breakfast from the dumbwaiter.

"I wish I'd thought of a dumbwaiter for Windward Hall," she said. "It's such a good idea."

126

"Make a note of that for our next renovation, in about forty years. By the way, Peter loves the house. He told me to tell you, and to ask you if you'd consider being the production designer for the film he wants to shoot there."

Susan laughed. "Tell him I'll consider it."

He finished breakfast and went back to the *Times*. There was a good-sized piece on the entertainment page about the explosions in Santa Monica and Coeur d'Alene, and Dr. Don Beverly Calhoun was interviewed. "I don't know why anyone would think we would be involved in such a thing," he said, "even if the movie is a scurrilous piece of trash, full of lies and distortions."

Stone went downstairs and faxed Peter the *Times* review. The phone rang.

"Hi, it's Eggers. It's Saturday, would you and Susan like to drive up to Connecticut with me? I've got all the closing documents, so we can take care of that."

"Why don't we meet you there? We can have lunch at the Mayflower Inn."

"Fine, I'll book us in. Shall we meet there at one o'clock?"

"Sounds good." He hung up and went to find Susan. She was sitting at her dressing table working on her laptop.

"I'm looking at the beta version of my

design program," she said.

"Would you like to try it out today on a charming New England house?"

"That sounds like fun."

"We'll leave here at eleven then, and bring an overnight bag, in case we decide to stay the night."

His phone rang. "Stone Barrington."

"Mr. Barrington, this is Dick Myers of the Associated Press. May I speak to your son, Peter?"

"I'm sorry, but Peter is on vacation, and he won't be available for interviews until he returns. Where are you calling from?"

"Chicago. May I know where he is? I just need to check a couple of facts, before we run our piece."

Stone looked at the caller ID; it was from an L.A. number, and he jotted it down. "I'm afraid that's classified. He's at a very secluded resort."

"Out West, is he?"

"I didn't say that. Out of the country would be more accurate. Goodbye."

"Mr. Barrington, it really is very important — to him as well as to me — to get in touch with him. I promise I won't invade his privacy."

"You want to invade his privacy to tell him you won't invade his privacy?"

"It's just fact-checking, really."

"Try him at his office in a couple of months." The man was still talking when he hung up. "Yeah, sure, you're from the AP," he said aloud.

At eleven, Stone put their bags into the Blaise, the French sports car that his friend Marcel duBois manufactured near Paris.

"I've read about these," Susan said, "and I've seen a couple in London, but I've never ridden in one."

"Then fasten your seat belt," Stone said before he pulled out of the garage and headed for the West Side Highway and the Sawmill River Parkway beyond. The sun was out and the trees were just starting to bud. They listened to classical music on the satellite radio and chatted.

Then, for the second or third time, Stone noticed a black SUV a couple of cars back that kept pulling into the left lane, as if to get a look at him.

"Something wrong?" Susan asked. "You keep checking your rearview mirror."

"Not a thing," Stone said, and picked up the pace. The SUV stuck with him.

They arrived at the Mayflower Inn and went in for lunch. "Excuse me a moment," he said to Susan. He went to the front desk.

"Hello, Mr. Barrington," the clerk said.

"Good afternoon. My son, Peter, isn't staying here, but I'd like to know if anyone inquires for him."

"Of course."

"I'll be in the restaurant. If someone asks for him, don't tell the person he isn't registered, but please send someone to get me."

"As you wish."

Stone rejoined Susan, and they went into the dining room, where Bill and Margo Eggers were waiting for them. Bill's wives kept getting younger, he thought. Introductions were made and lunch ordered.

They were between courses when a young man came to the table. "Excuse me, Mr. Barrington," he said, "but there's a man at the front desk asking for Peter Barrington."

"Thank you," Stone said. He excused himself and left the dining room. A beefy man of about forty was waiting at the desk. "Good afternoon. My name is Barrington. Come with me," Stone said, leading the way, "and we'll find some privacy." He led the man into the little library off the main lobby. "Now," he said, "who are you?"

"Uh . . ." the man began, then stopped. "Never you mind who I am."

"Let's see some ID."

"I don't have to show you nothing."

Stone took the man's wrist, spun him around, shoved it behind his back between the shoulder blades, and bent him over the back of a sofa.

"Let me go, you son of a bitch!"

Stone found a wallet in his hip pocket and flipped it over.

"Ah, Mr. William Givers of Los Angeles," he said. "I thought you might be from the Associated Press. Now tell me, what do you want from Peter Barrington?"

"I don't want anything from him."

Stone pushed the hand up farther and got a groan of pain from him. He continued to flip through the wallet with his free hand until he found a card. "What a surprise," he said. "You're the director of public relations, New York, for the Chosen Few, and you told me only this morning that you were from the AP."

"You're going to be sorry you did this," the man said.

Stone reached around the man, feeling his waist, and found a handgun in a holster. He extracted it. "Is this a common tool for a director of public relations?" he asked.

"None of your fucking business."

"Funny, looking through your wallet, I

didn't find a Connecticut carry permit. If you have one, show it to me." He let go of the man's arm and stepped back, while popping out the magazine and clearing the breech.

The man backed away from him. "Stay away from me."

"You've got it all backwards," Stone said. "You stay away from me. As it happens, I have both a Connecticut and a New York carry permit, so maybe I should keep the gun for you." He picked up the magazine and thumbed the cartridges until it was empty, then slapped it back into the pistol.

The man turned and ran from the library. Stone picked up the cartridges and dropped them into his pocket, then he walked quickly through the lobby, slipping the gun also into his pocket, and out onto the front porch, just in time to see a black SUV departing. It had a New York plate, and he jotted down the number, then he went back into the dining room. "Sorry about that," he said, sitting down to his main course.

"Anything wrong?" Eggers asked.

"Not anymore," Stone replied.

19

They drove back to Stone's house in two cars and went inside. Susan had a look around with Margo and took a lot of pictures with her iPhone, then they sat down at the kitchen table, and Susan got her laptop set up. They began looking at rooms, changing the colors and fabrics with her computer program. Stone went upstairs and packed what few clothes he had there into a suitcase, then took it down to the car.

As he was opening the trunk the black SUV drove past. Stone got out his phone, looked up the number of his friend Dan Brady, who was commandant of the Connecticut State Police.

"Hey, Stone, what's up?"

Stone told him about Peter's new movie.

"Yeah, I saw about the explosions on the news."

"They have an operative in New York who called me this morning, pretending to be from the AP, looking for Peter, then followed me to Washington this morning. I took a gun away from him, but he's still following me. I'm at my house, and he just drove by in a black Grand Cherokee with a New York plate." He gave Dan the number.

"Do you still have the gun?"

"Yes."

"Stay where you are. I'll call the Litchfield troop and get a car over there, then get back to you."

"Thanks, Dan, you have the number and the street address."

"Sure."

They hung up and Stone went back into the house. As he was going inside, a car pulled up and a woman got out, carrying a briefcase. "Can you tell me where to find Bill Eggers?" she asked.

"Right this way."

Eggers greeted her, took her into the dining room, and told her to get set up. "Are you ready to close, Stone?"

"You betcha." Stone went into the dining room and he and Eggers signed the many documents necessary to close a real estate sale, then Eggers handed him a cashier's check for two million dollars.

"Thank you very much," Stone said. "I wish you a happy time in the house."

They were in the kitchen when the doorbell rang, and Stone went to answer it. Two uniformed state troopers stood on the porch with William Givers, handcuffed, between them.

"I'm Sergeant Miller," one of them said. "Mr. Barrington?"

"That's me."

"I understand that you have a firearm that you took from this gentleman?"

"Correct, except for the gentleman part." Stone took the weapon and its cartridges from his pocket and handed them to Miller. "It's been cleared."

Miller cleared it again himself, then turned to Givers. "William Givers, you are under arrest for the unlawful possession of a firearm in the State of Connecticut. You will come with us. Thank you, Mr. Barrington. We'll be in touch to get a written statement."

"I'll fax you one on Monday," Stone said. He went back into the house and took Eggers on a tour of the house's systems, then called the security company and gave them the names of the new owners.

Stone and Eggers watched a football game on TV, while Susan and Margo continued working on the computer. As it grew late, Stone booked a room at the Mayflower and a dinner table at the West Street Grill, in Litchfield. The ladies joined them for a drink, then Stone and Susan went to change.

They were having dinner in Litchfield when Stone's cell phone vibrated.

"Hello?"

"Hi, it's Dan. I thought you'd like to know that Givers was bailed out by a local attorney a few minutes ago."

"No arraignment?"

"The attorney brought a judge with him. Givers will have to make a court appearance on Tuesday. Where are you?"

"In Litchfield."

"So is Givers, so watch yourself."

"Did you give him his gun back?"

"No, and we kept the shotgun we found in his car, too, and the two boxes of ammo for the handgun and the shotgun, or riot gun, I should say; it has a short barrel."

"So much for public relations," Stone said.

Brady laughed. "Yeah."

"I'll fax you an affidavit on Monday morning. Will I need to make an appearance?"

"Not unless he's tried. I expect he'll plead to a lesser charge, pay a fine, and walk."

"Well, I'm glad to have caused him some

trouble, anyway."

"Do you think you've heard the last of these people?"

"I doubt it, but I'm leaving the country at the end of next week, and they won't know where I am."

"Good idea. Let 'em cool off."

"Thanks, Dan, and take care of yourself."

"Same to you. Thanks for helping us get him off the street, at least for a while."

Stone hung up and went back to his dinner.

20

They spent a lazy Sunday morning in bed, watching the political shows and reading the *Times.* "How'd you and Margo do with your computer program?"

"Very well, with only a couple of glitches, and I've already e-mailed that news to the software team. Margo and I are going to meet at your house in a couple of days and nail down the materials she'll need, and my team will ship them to her late next week. They'll get to work on the draperies, too, and she'll have them in about three weeks. A firm in New York I've worked with before will do the painting and installations, and we'll find an upholsterer to redo some of the furniture."

"So long-distance design works, huh?"

"I am absolutely delighted with the computer program, and with the client's willingness to make decisions from looking at pictures on a screen. This is going to make me a lot more productive."

"I'm glad to hear it, if it will make it easier for you to come to New York."

"It just might," she replied.

They had lunch downstairs and then left for New York.

They drove back to I-84 West, and as they crossed the state line, they passed a black BMW SUV, parked on the shoulder. Stone watched in his mirror as the driver started the car and pulled into traffic behind them.

"What is it?" Susan asked.

"Another black SUV. Let's see if he follows us when we get onto I-684." The SUV followed. Stone called Dan Brady.

"Sorry to trouble you again, Dan, but I've got another one on my tail, this time a black BMW SUV."

"Where are you?"

"In New York State, and I don't know anyone on the state police here."

"I'll call somebody, and they'll be in touch. What's your position?"

"On I-684 South, middle lane, coming up on the Hardscrabble Road exit. I'll be turning off at the Sawmill, at Exit 5."

"What are you driving?"

"A Blaise. I hope they'll know what that is."

"I'm on it," Dan said, then hung up.

Stone tried driving faster, then slower, and the BMW kept pace, always two or three cars back. As he left the interstate and turned onto the Sawmill his phone rang. "Yes?"

"Mr. Barrington, this is Lieutenant Schwartz of the New York State Police. We hear from Colonel Brady in Connecticut that you're driving a Blaise and being pursued by a black BMW SUV. Is that correct?"

"That is correct."

"We should have eyes on you and him within about five minutes."

"I'm on the Sawmill now, passing Katonah."

"Stand by." He was quiet for a moment, then came back. "We've got you," he said. "Pull off the Sawmill at the next exit, and I'll have him stopped there. You stop, too."

"Lieutenant, your trooper should know that the last one who followed me was armed with a handgun and a shotgun, both loaded."

"I heard that from Colonel Brady," he said. "We'll have two cars on the stop. Slow down to forty when you're off the Sawmill, and stay on this line with me."

"Will do."

Stone saw an exit coming up and put on his blinker. He left the Sawmill and slowed to forty mph; so did the BMW. As he watched in the mirror he saw two New York State Police cars coming up from behind. One passed the BMW, and the other pulled in behind. Once they had him boxed, their lights came on, and they pulled him onto the shoulder.

"Stay in your car," Schwartz said.

"Yes, sir." He watched in his mirror as two troopers pulled a man from the BMW, while two other troopers stood behind his car, weapons drawn. He saw the man being frisked and relieved of a handgun, then cuffed. One of the troopers then opened the rear door and removed what looked like an assault rifle.

"That's it," Schwartz said, "he's in custody, and he doesn't have a carry license. You may proceed on your way now, and we'll be in touch if we need you further."

"Thank you very much, Lieutenant, and goodbye." Stone made a U-turn and got back on the Sawmill.

"You seem to have very good relations with the police," Susan said, "and in two states. I'm impressed."

"Dan Brady did all the work," Stone said.

"Do you think that man really meant you harm?"

"I don't know, but I don't think he was armed to protect himself from me."

21

Stone was at his desk the following morning when Dino called. "I'm messengering something to you," he said. "I want you to read it immediately, then messenger it back to me."

"All right." Joan walked in with a package. "I think it's already here." Stone unwrapped it and found an FBI file about an inch thick, with the name Donald Beverly Calhoun on it.

"Read it and call me back," Dino said.

Stone started to read.

It was nearly lunchtime when he finished and called Dino. "Thank you," he said.

"You read it all?"

"Yes. How did you get it?"

"I called the director at home, and he had it copied and sent to me."

"Do you mind if I copy it?"

"No, but keep quiet about it. What were

your impressions?"

"I'm amazed at the guy's ability to skate on thin ice without ever falling through. I mean, once in a while the ice cracks, and he dips a leg into the water, but then he manages to get up and skate on."

"What I can't figure out," Dino said, "is what he wants. I mean, if he just wants to make money, he's doing that with his books and 'documentaries,' for which he's getting forty bucks a pop and not splitting the take with an agent or publisher. The guy's printing money."

"And he's doing it all under the radar," Stone pointed out. "You hardly ever see anything about him in the papers and TV programs I watch."

"Except when he has a magazine writer murdered, or somebody makes a movie about somebody a lot like him."

"He's trying hard to find Peter and Ben, and he's having me followed by armed men," Stone said, and told Dino about his experiences over the weekend.

"You did the right thing, calling Dan Brady," Dino said. "Maybe if you keep getting his people arrested, he'll back off."

"I hope you're right. We'll lose them when Susan and I leave for England later in the week. I hope I'm right about that, too."

"Me, too, since Viv is going with you."

"I'll have Joan send the file back to you right away," Stone said. They said goodbye, and he buzzed Joan, who came in. He handed her the file. "Please copy this — the whole thing — then messenger it back to Dino."

Joan weighed it in her hands. "The whole thing, huh?"

"All of it, and make two copies."

"Okay, boss." She left, then he heard the Xerox machine laboring away.

Susan was working on Margo Eggers's house, so he had Helene send lunch up to her, then made a date with Mike Freeman at the Four Seasons Grill Room.

Over lunch, Stone told Mike about what was going on. "Have you ever heard of this guy Calhoun?"

"Here and there over the years, but you're right, he skates on thin ice remarkably well."

Stone pulled a wrapped package from under the table and handed it to him. "This is his FBI file. Don't ask how I got it. Read it, then send it back to me."

Mike accepted the package. "You know what I find most remarkable about Calhoun?"

"What?"

145

"Most of these — let's call them tribal leaders — live somewhere like on a mountaintop in Idaho, or some lost ranch in the Mojave Desert, but Dr. Don's business and his people are based in a major American metropolis."

"Hiding in plain sight."

"Exactly. I wonder if his neighbors even know he's there."

"I certainly wouldn't want him in my neighborhood."

"I think you ought to let me put some people on your house," Mike said. "I don't like people in black SUVs running around with loaded illegal weapons."

"Well, nobody took a shot at me. In fact, I accosted the first guy when he asked for Peter at the front desk of the Mayflower. He didn't think he was stepping on my toes, he just thought Peter was there."

"Why did he think Peter was there?"

"Because he followed me there from New York. I'd already told him on the phone that Peter was on vacation at a resort, so I guess he thought I was going to see him, not selling my house to Bill Eggers."

"You know, I would have bought your house, if I'd known it was on the market."

"I'm flattered, but I never put it on the market. I just told Eggers about it, and he

146

bit — or, at least, his wife did."

They shook hands and parted. In the late afternoon, Stone's second copy of Dr. Don's FBI file came back to him from Mike Freeman.

22

During the week Susan had her meeting with Bill Eggers, Julian Whately, and half a dozen other people from Woodman & Weld. She came home aglow.

"That was a real eye-opener for me," she said.

"What did they recommend?"

"They want me to expand at every level of my business — to hire a publicist to 'heat up' my name, as they put it, to hire four people over the next year to supervise projects and report to me. They want me to buy the building in Wandsworth where my upholsterers are based and turn another floor into a draperies and fabrics workshop, and they'll arrange financing. They've suggested that I design my own line of upholstered furniture and develop a line of slipcovers that fit the pieces. They want me to hire a team of people to go around England and France, buying antique furniture and objets d'art and use another floor of the building to warehouse them. They reckon I can get quadruple what I pay for them, if I buy judiciously. And once this is all working, they want me to do a deal with a chain of high-end shops, who would carry my fabrics, towels, and bathroom accessories. The mind boggles!"

"May I make a suggestion?"

"Of course."

"Hire somebody really good to be your chief operating officer, so you can spend your time designing, instead of managing."

"What a good idea! I'm going to be a very busy woman!"

Stone winced. Had he created a monster? She certainly wasn't going to have much time for him.

"They also think that being the production designer on Peter's film would be a wonderful showcase, and I've already done the perfect house for the project — yours!"

She left him to go and make phone calls to London.

Very early on Friday morning, Fred collected Viv Bacchetti from her apartment, then came for Stone and Susan. They were at Teterboro before rush hour, and were soon taxiing to the runway. Pat Frank's people had already done his flight planning and were predicting winds that would take him to Windward Hall nonstop, after St. John's.

The two women sat in the rear of the airplane and chatted, until Susan had to make satphone calls to her office. They refueled at St. John's, Newfoundland, then set off for England. Once Stone was at flight level 410, he picked up the predicted 100-knot tailwinds, and the range ring showed Windward well within its boundaries. Settled en route, Stone read the *Times,* then opened a book of *New York Times* Sunday crosswords, the perfect long-distance flying companion: look at a clue, write down the answer, do an instrument scan. He got into a rhythm.

They flew across the Atlantic, and ATC vectored him to the GPS instrument approach. They touched down at dusk, ready to stretch their legs.

Stan met them, towing a trailer for their luggage behind the Land Rover, and drove them to the house. They joined the kids and the Barnetts in the library for before-dinner drinks, then adjourned for Stone's first dinner in his new dining room.

Peter and Susan sat next to each other and talked animatedly about his upcoming film. He had completed a first draft of the script and was having the office make a copy for her to study and come up with ideas.

They were back in the dining room for brandy and coffee when Stone's cell phone vibrated on his belt. He checked the caller ID and found it blocked. "Hello?"

"It's your neighbor across the river," Felicity said.

"Hang on." Stone excused himself from the conversation, went to a corner of the room, and sank into a chair. "How are you? I was sorry not to see you at Charles's big party."

"And I was sorry to miss it, but the Muddle East claimed that whole weekend. I understand he's returning from his honeymoon early next week."

"I hope they had a good time," Stone said.

"I expect so."

Stone thought he detected something troubled in her voice. "Is there something you want to tell me, Felicity?"

She took a deep breath. "Well, yes, there is. It appears that you're going to have some less-than-desirable neighbors, unless we can do something about it."

"Neighbors where?"

"Apparently, Sir Richard Curtis's widow, next door to you, has been approached by estate agents and is considering selling the property. She had thought to sell it to an institutional buyer, like a school or perhaps even a nunnery."

"Of those choices I think I would prefer a nunnery for a neighbor," Stone said. "At least they would live quietly."

"At the moment, that seems the most unlikely buyer," Felicity said. "As it turned out, the estate agents she consulted had had a request in hand for several weeks from a different kind of organization, which now seems, to the agents, an ideal buyer."

"What kind of organization?"

"A cult, I believe."

Stone sat up straight. "What is its name?"

"The Chosen Few."

23

Stone froze. "What did you say?"

"A cult, called the Chosen Few. Do you know them?"

"Better than I'd like to," Stone said. He explained about Peter's film and the recent brushes with the group. "I read their leader's FBI file — Dr. Don Beverly Calhoun — and it was not pretty."

"Perhaps I should speak to the Home Secretary about them," Felicity said. "He might find them undesirable enough to keep them out of the country."

"What a good idea," Stone said.

"In the meantime, however, I think we should direct our attention to torpedoing any offer they might make for the Curtis estate. I know the widow, Glynnis. Perhaps I'll give her a call and alert her to the nature of the Chosen Few."

"I would be very grateful if you could do that. Will you let me know her reaction?"

"Certainly."

"I must go, now. Peter, Ben Bacchetti, and their entourage are staying here, and I have to let them entertain me."

"I'll speak to you tomorrow. Good night."

"Good night." Stone hung up.

"Anything wrong, Dad?" Peter asked.

"Not yet," Stone replied.

Stone was finally able to lure Susan into the master suite for the night and for a late breakfast, as well. They were tired from their flight and had slept in.

"I like your new beds," she said.

"You are welcome there anytime at all."

The phone rang. "Hello?"

"Stone," Felicity said, "I've spoken to Glynnis Curtis, and the news is not good. She learned after Richard's death that he was not as well off as she had thought — bad investments, or something — and she feels that the only way she can secure her future is to sell the estate as soon as possible. The Chosen Few people saw the property yesterday, and this morning she received a written offer of twenty-two million pounds."

"Did you mention the possibility of the group's presence being found unacceptable to the government?"

"I did, and she doesn't give a damn. They'll pay cash and complete quickly, and then it will be their problem."

"Then what can we do? Can we object to the sale?"

"Possibly, if there is something in the zoning laws that would make them undesirable, but I know of an estate not ten miles away that is occupied by a religious sect something like your Amish, in the States. I think there is only one way to stop them in their tracks."

"And what is that?"

"Buy it yourself."

"Christ in heaven, Felicity! I can't do that."

"Of course you can, Stone. When you were consulting with my service some years back I ordered a background investigation of your character and assets, so I know what you inherited from Arrington, and I know that your capital has grown since that time. I also know that you are the sole trustee of your son's trust, which is even larger than your holdings, so you could buy it as an investment for the trust."

"Let me get back to you," Stone said.

"I'll pick you up in an hour. We have an appointment with Lady Curtis to view the place." She hung up.

155

Stone put down the phone.

"You look as if someone has just punched you in the gut," Susan said. "What's wrong?"

"You're not going to believe this," Stone said.

Felicity showed up on time in a Jaguar saloon, and they got in. "Now listen to me, Stone," Felicity said, spinning the car around and pointing it down the driveway, "I know you don't want to buy this place, but you've got to pretend to be interested, so that we can slow down Glynnis's decision-making process. She's frightened of her future and very vulnerable, so the offer from the cult seems to her like a lifeline. She has to be persuaded to think there is another way forward. Do you understand?"

"I understand," Stone said, "but I am *not* going to buy this place."

They turned onto the main road and drove for a mile or so, then turned into a drive marked by an elegant gateway. High stone walls stretched away in both directions.

"If that wall goes down to the river on both sides of the estate," Susan said, "it's a million pounds' worth of masonry."

"I'm happy for Lady Curtis," Stone said.

The house came into view, and it was impressive. "It's half again as large as Windward Hall," he said.

"Twice as large," Susan replied, "perhaps more."

They pulled to a stop in front of the house and climbed the stairs to the front door and rang the bell. Lady Curtis herself opened the door, and introductions were made.

"I'm sorry I haven't had the opportunity to meet you sooner, Mr. Barrington," she said, "but circumstances intervened."

"I'm very glad to be able to meet you now, Lady Curtis," he replied.

"Let me give you the ten-shilling tour," she said, "and then we'll have some lunch."

They followed her through a succession of elegant rooms filled with fine paintings and sculptures. The wallpaper was peeling here and there, and the paint could have been better. The style of decorating was heavy for Stone's taste. There was a huge drawing room, a large library, a conservatory, a billiards room, a writing room, and a music room, with a concert grand piano and a harp. Then they toured the second and third floors; Stone quickly lost count of the number of bedrooms. They also toured the lower level, where there was an Edwardian-era kitchen and servants hall, plus quarters for the help. The utility rooms were clean, and the equipment looked serviceable, if old.

They went back to the conservatory, where a cold lunch was served by uniformed staff. At one point Lady Curtis was called to the phone, and Susan tugged at Stone's sleeve.

"I told you that I am meeting with a possible client, a hotel group, on Monday."

"I remember," Stone said.

"I think I could interest them in this place," she said, "if it came to them thoroughly renovated. They are known to prefer properties in a move-in condition."

"How much to renovate the place?" Stone asked.

"A wild guess? Five million pounds, if we don't have to replace all the bathroom fixtures. I think the old ones could be refinished, and they add charm. Have you visited Cliveden, the former home of the Astors?"

"Yes, a couple of times."

"A renovation much like that, albeit on a smaller scale."

"Another good reason not to buy the place," Stone said.

Felicity had been listening closely. "I like the way you think, Susan. Now, when Glynnis comes back, let me do the talking. You, in particular, Stone, shut up."

Lady Curtis returned and apologized for her absence. "That was the estate agents," she said. "They're pressing for an acceptance."

"Glynnis," Felicity said, "I urge you not to be rushed into this deal. The buyers are unsavory people, and I believe that if you can give me a week or so, I might be able to come up with a better buyer, perhaps even a better offer. Have you signed an agreement to be represented by the estate agents?"

"Not yet; they're pressing for that, too."

"You would clear more from the sale if you didn't have to pay their commission."

Lady Curtis brightened. "A good point, Felicity, yes, I'll give you a week to see what you can do."

They thanked her for the tour and lunch, then excused themselves.

"That is an *extraordinary* property," Susan said, as soon as they were in the car. "I could make it into the most spectacular country hotel in Europe. What do you think, Stone?"

"I think you could certainly do that, if you can interest your hotelier in the property."

"Did I mention that the estate is some two

159

hundred acres and that there are at least a dozen cottages on the property?" Felicity asked. "Those could be done up and rented, as well."

"Thank you, Felicity," Stone said, "but no dice."

"I'll take that as a maybe," Felicity replied, gunning the Jaguar.

24

They got back to the house, and Stone took Felicity into the library, where the gang awaited, and introduced her to everyone.

"Where have you been?" Peter asked.

"We've just seen the most glorious house," Susan said, "and it's right next door." She told him about the place.

"I want to see it," Peter said.

Stone sat up straight. "Why?"

"It sounds interesting. I might find a way to work it into the script."

"I'll take you back right now," Felicity said. "Let me phone Lady Curtis."

"But you haven't even had lunch," Stone said to Peter.

"Yes, we have, we'd just finished when you arrived. Do you want to come with us?"

"There isn't room in the car," Stone said.

Peter and Ben and their girls left with Felicity.

"I don't like the way this is going," Stone

said to Susan.

"Why ever not? They'll enjoy seeing it."

"You're all going to gang up on me. I can see it coming."

"Nonsense. Read a magazine or something. There's a stack of *Country Life* over there."

Stone picked up a magazine and found it filled with country estates for sale. "The last thing I want to read," he said, flinging it across the room.

Billy Barnett spoke up. "Is the lady you just introduced to us, Dame Felicity Devonshire, the head of MI6?"

"She is," Stone said, "and she missed her calling: she should have been a real estate agent."

"I know the style of decoration is out of date," Susan said, "not at all what you like, but when I'm done, you'll love it."

"I don't have to love it — your hotelier prospective client will, no doubt. At least, I hope he does."

"I've had another idea, too," she said.

Stone threw up his hands. "Can we change the subject, please? I've already heard too much about that house."

"As you wish," she said frostily. "If you'll excuse me, I have some work to do. Let me know when it's dinnertime." She walked briskly out of the room.

"Now I've done it," Stone groaned. "She won't speak to me for the rest of the weekend."

Peter came back, raving about Curtis House. "It's incredible! I wouldn't want to live there, but wow! What a property! Did you see the cottages?"

"No," Stone said, "and I don't think the house would be a good investment for your trust."

"No? I think Susan could do it up, and we could sell it at a very nice profit."

"That would be a very large bet."

"One I could afford to lose," Peter pointed out.

"That's not a good investment attitude, it's a roll of the dice."

"I like the fact that it's available right away."

"Take a few deep breaths, Peter."

Felicity came into the room. "I've just spoken with the Home Secretary," she said, "and told him about this Calhoun person. He'd already heard about him from MI5, who have reported to him that the man is on his way to London as we speak. He's agreed to declare him an undesirable person and have him stopped at the airport and

163

sent back on the next flight. Both Heathrow and Gatwick have been alerted."

"Now that is very good news," Stone said. "I'll bet he was coming to look at Curtis House."

"That could very well be — he'd be mad to buy the place sight unseen."

"The bad news is, he *is* mad," Stone said. "Or, at least, he sounds that way. Did I tell you I saw the FBI file on the man? I'll have it sent to you, if you like."

"Oh, yes, please," Felicity said. "I'll need all the ammunition I can get to persuade the secretary to ban him permanently."

Stone called Joan and asked her to copy the file and FedEx it to Felicity. "You'll have it Monday morning," he told her.

"I can't wait to read it. Where's Susan gone?"

"She said she had some work to do."

"You annoyed her with your attitude about the house, didn't you?"

"Probably. You two have got Peter on my back about it now."

"Oh, he loved it, and Lady Curtis loved him. A match made in heaven."

"I'm not sure you've got your geography right," Stone said.

Susan came into the library. "I've just spoken with my assistant and there's some work I have to do in London before my meeting on Monday. Could you ask Stan to drive me? My bags are all packed."

"Of course," Stone said, and nothing else he could say to her made a difference.

25

Stone, knowing he had gone too far, e-mailed Susan:

My Dear Susan, I want to apologize for making such an argument about Curtis House. I overreacted, and I did not mean to make you the brunt of that. The next time I refuse to buy it, I will be kinder.

He got an e-mail back, saying:

I am at fault for harrying you about the house. The next time I urge you to buy it I will use fewer words.

Stone had breakfast in bed, as usual, and read the Sunday papers. He was going to have to find out how to get the *New York Times* delivered in England, even if it was a day late.

There was a knock on his bedroom door.

"Come in!"

Peter came into the room. "Ben had a thought last night that might play into your decision about whether to buy Curtis House."

Stone almost yelled, but caught himself. "Yes?"

"If I use the big house in my film, Ben thinks we can charge a substantial part of the renovations to my budget, without raising the studio's hackles."

"That's certainly an attractive idea," Stone said, "but, speaking as a board member, I think you should be frank with Centurion about what you're doing and get specific approvals in advance of building that into your budget. It might also help to have Susan prepare a room-by-room budget. You certainly won't be using the whole house. Also, you shouldn't plunge ahead on your script until you know who is going to own the house. I don't think Dr. Don would be open to your using it."

"Good point, Dad. Are you getting out of bed today?"

"I'm considering it."

"Why don't you and I take a ride after lunch?"

"Horse or Porsche?"

"I was thinking horse. Nobody else seems

much interested. Hattie has discovered your Steinway, and she wants to work on some ideas she has for the score of the film, and I think Ben plans to spend the afternoon screwing his girl."

"You're on, kiddo."

They rode across the meadow in front of the house and into the woods, along a well-beaten trail. It was cool under the trees, and they slowed to a walk to better enjoy the air.

"Dad, what's that?" Peter asked. He was pointing at a small structure.

"That," Stone said, "is the hermitage, where the hermit lived."

"Hermit?"

Stone turned his horse and rode slowly toward the little house, while he told Peter about the killing of Sir Richard Curtis and the confession and suicide of the hermit, Wilfred Burns. He gave him all the background on the service in the Royal Marines of Burns, Curtis, and Sir Charles Bourne.

"That's fascinating," Peter said as he dismounted and tied his reins to a bush. "I think I can use that story."

Stone tied his horse, and they tried the door to the house. It was unlocked, and they walked in. Stone had expected a hovel, and he was surprised to see how well the space was used and how neat the place was. It was, essentially, one room; there was a kitchenette in a corner, a woodstove, a small desk, and a single comfortable chair. There were built-in bookcases holding volumes that seemed mostly about military history. There was a tiny cupboard that held some military uniforms and a Squadron mess kit, along with some rougher clothing, and a sleeping loft had been built at one end, with a small bathroom underneath.

"This is what I call simple living," Peter said. "I don't think I could ever get along with so few possessions."

"Nor I," Stone said, "but I admire him for doing it. I think it must be part of his penance for the behavior that ruined his career."

"What did the police think was the brigadier's motive for killing Richard Curtis?" Peter asked.

"I don't know, and the police inspector never mentioned one. His suicide seemed to bring the investigation to a screeching halt, and when I last spoke to Inspector Holmes, I thought I detected a note of relief in his voice."

"Are you going to seek out a new hermit for the place?"

"No, I think I'll wait and see if one comes to me."

They had a look around the exterior and found a shed containing a couple of chain saws and some hand tools.

"He earned his keep here as a woodcutter," Stone explained to Peter.

They went back to their horses and mounted up, then rode on. As they passed within sight of the airfield, a twin-engine Piper Navajo came in and touched down, and Sir Charles and the new Lady Bourne got out, as Stan arrived with the Land Rover.

Stone rode over to meet them and introduced Peter. "I hope the honeymoon went well," he said. Charles, he thought, looked a little tired and perhaps a bit thinner, but then, the groom was supposed to be worn out after the honeymoon.

"We had a wonderful time, Stone," Elizabeth said, "and Marie was very kind to us, as well. We can't thank you enough."

They got into the Land Rover and drove toward Charles's cottage, and the airplane started up, took off, and headed south, toward France.

Stone and Peter rode on, passing the cemetery and the Norman church beyond.

They had a good view of Curtis Hall from there.

"Why don't we jump that wall and ride around the Curtis estate?" Peter asked.

"I think it would be more neighborly to ask permission first," Stone said, and as they watched, Lady Curtis came out the front door with four people who, somehow, looked American. She waved at Stone and Peter, and they waved back, then she beckoned to them and waved her arm in a sweep, as if to say, "Come ride on my property."

They jumped the horses over the wall and walked on, as the group got into a limousine and drove away, passing a few yards ahead of their path.

"They looked American," Peter said.

"I thought so, too," Stone replied, "and the tall one looked like pictures I've seen of Dr. Don Beverly Calhoun."

"Oh, shit," Peter said.

26

They spent a good two hours covering the whole of the Curtis estate, which was indeed larger than Stone's property, and then they rode along the Beaulieu River toward the dock of Windward Hall. Stone's cell phone vibrated.

"Hello?"

"It's Felicity."

"I know what you're going to tell me."

"Okay, what?"

"That Dr. Don Beverly Calhoun somehow got into the country."

"How could you know that?"

"Because I just saw him leaving Curtis Hall."

"He flew private, into Biggin Hill."

"I figured."

"We didn't cover private airfields; there are too many."

"I figured. Why don't you get your friend the Home Secretary to throw him out of the country?"

"Oh, no, it's easy to block someone from entering, and that way, you deny him the media, but arresting and deporting him is much more complicated and could even be appealed, and we'd have the papers and TV all over us."

"I see your point."

"Did you actually see Calhoun and Glynnis together?"

"I saw her saying goodbye to him and three others, then they got into a limo and passed within a few yards of us."

"Did they look as though they had concluded a deal?"

"Oh, come on, Felicity, what sort of look is that?"

"Oh, all right, I'll call her. Goodbye."

Stone hung up. "The river runs down to the Solent," he said to Peter. "Very convenient for boating."

"Are you going to get a boat?"

"I don't have a crew — maybe a powerboat."

"Another Hinckley?"

"That's a good thought — it could be shipped to Southampton. I'm not really in the mood to research British boats. I'd know what I'm getting with a Hinckley."

"Good. The next time we visit, I'll expect

a Hinckley ride."

"It sounds to me as though you're going to be spending the rest of the year here, and why not? You can finish your script, do a deal with a British production house for a crew and equipment, and get your casting done. What sort of schedule are you thinking about?"

"I'll have to work it up. We'll need to finish the script, do production drawings, and run it by the studio. Then preproduction and a few weeks of shooting. We'd want to do postproduction at home, since we have all the equipment in our offices. I think we could be ready for release in December, in time for Academy Awards qualification and screenings."

"Sounds like you've given it a lot of thought."

"I've hardly thought about anything else. It would be a new experience, having a film go from inspiration to completion so quickly."

"Maybe I'll figure out a way to get my New York work done over here. I'd love to watch your film happen. I'd promise not to get in the way."

"Nonsense, you've been nothing but helpful. This film wouldn't have happened but for you."

"You sound as if it's already made."

They were back at Windward Hall in time for tea in the library, which turned out to be more of a production meeting, as Peter brought Ben and Billy up to date on what he'd seen and planned.

Felicity called again. "It's all right, Glynnis hasn't accepted the Calhoun offer yet."

"Swell."

"You don't sound pleased."

"It's nothing to do with me."

"So you're looking forward to having Dr. Don and his tribe as neighbors?"

"You have a point."

"You'd better get interested."

"I'll think about it, I promise."

"That's all I ask."

"The hell it is. You won't be happy until I've written another enormous check."

"You know me so well." She hung up.

The following day Stone was about to sit down for lunch when Susan Blackburn called. "Are you sitting down?"

"Oh, God."

"My hotelier prospective client has not the slightest interest in having a country hotel in his portfolio of properties."

"He sounds like me."

175

"All too much. In thinking about this, though, it occurred to me that we both know another hotelier."

"And who would that be?"

"You."

"Me, a hotelier?"

"You're building your third in Rome right now."

"That's Marcel. I'm just a kibitzer."

"Well, kibitz your way into getting Marcel aboard."

Stone thought about that.

"I take your silence as consideration."

"Oh, all right, I'll call him."

"I'd like to hear the result of that conversation quite soon."

"I'll call him now." Stone said goodbye, then dialed Marcel duBois's number in Rome.

"Pronto."

"You sound very Italian."

"Stone! How are you?"

"Very well, thank you. I'm in England, where I've bought a country place."

"Word has reached me. Is it beautiful?"

"Very. Have you ever thought of having a country Arrington?"

"Oh, yes, I've looked in France, but I haven't found the right place."

"I believe I may have found the right place

in England, and right next door to me." He told Marcel about Curtis House.

"That sounds very interesting."

"There's a landing field on my property. Why don't you hop over here tomorrow and see the place?"

"Tomorrow? I can do that."

"And stay the night with me — longer, if you can."

"One night, perhaps."

Stone gave him the landing particulars. "I'll see you tomorrow, around ten AM, then."

"I look forward."

27

Stone called Susan. "All right, I've taken your suggestion: Marcel is coming tomorrow, which means you have to come down tonight so we can give him a tour of the Curtis estate early in the day."

"I can do that," Susan said.

He hung up and called Felicity, explained things to her, and asked her to tell Glynnis to expect callers in the morning. He hung up feeling the first twinges of excitement about Curtis House.

Marcel and Lady Curtis got on immediately and well. She showed them the house, top to bottom, while Susan took photographs with a digital camera, and there followed another lunch in the conservatory. After coffee, Marcel begged to have a moment alone with Stone. "You say she has an offer for twenty-two million pounds?"

"Yes."

"Then we'll offer her twenty-two million five?"

"Good."

"To include the furnishings?"

"We can ask. If she doesn't go for that, we can have Susan go through the house and designate pieces for us to make an offer on."

"Agreed."

They went back into the conservatory. "Lady Curtis," Marcel said, "I am pleased to offer you twenty-two million, five hundred thousand pounds for your house and its contents."

Lady Curtis didn't bat an eye. "I will accept your offer, but excluding the art in the drawing room, the library, and the master suite."

Marcel glanced at Stone and got a tiny nod. "Done." He stood up and took her hand. "I will have a contract and a check for ten percent of the purchase price in your hands tomorrow morning, and we will close as quickly as our respective lawyers will allow us."

"Oh, good," she said.

Marcel gave her hand a kiss, and they were gone.

"I don't believe it," Susan said when they were in the car. "Do you always do business so quickly?"

"Delay and doubt are always partners," Marcel replied. "And you will be our designer for the Curtis Arrington?"

"I will be delighted. I have enough photos to begin work tomorrow."

"I have a thought," Stone said. He told her about Peter's desire to work in England until his film was done. "We have a dozen unoccupied staff bedrooms at Windward Hall," he said. "The staff, over the years, has moved either into the cottages or into Beaulieu. Why don't you make your first design job converting those rooms into work space for Peter's crowd and for you? The two of you can collaborate."

"And I will turn the servants' rooms at Curtis House into hotel rooms," Marcel said. "If we include the cottages, we'll have forty-odd guest rooms to sell."

"I'm going to have to start hiring those people your firm recommended, Stone," Susan said. "And I'm going to make an offer on the building in Wandsworth for our shops. I've had a word with my bankers already."

"You know," Stone said, "a month ago none of this was real. Now we're going to be giving work to a couple of hundred talented people for the rest of the year, at least, and early next year there will be a record on film of what we did."

"It's breathtaking," Susan said.

The news of the acquisition of Curtis House was met with glee by Peter and his entourage, and a celebratory dinner was instantly arranged.

Stone called Felicity. "It's done," he said.

"I know, I've already talked to Glynnis."

"You see how you manipulate me?"

"*Manipulate* is a vulgar word. I simply offer you irresistible opportunities."

"Come to dinner tonight?"

"Oh, how I wish I could, but the Muddle East occupies me nonstop."

The cook at Windward Hall, on six hours' notice, shopped, cooked, and served dinner for nine people as if it were an everyday matter, and Stone plundered his new cellars for wines that would please Marcel. Everyone went to bed happy, especially Stone, who was relieved to have Susan back in his bed, if only for a night. Perhaps he could persuade her to make it two, or even longer.

The following morning, Susan, Peter, and Ben toured the empty servants' quarters below, and Susan drew up specifications for the electrician to beef up the wiring and Wi-Fi arrangements for the rooms and made a list of desks and chairs to order from London.

And in a London hotel Dr. Don Beverly Calhoun took the news of the loss of Curtis House with ill grace, firing his estate agents.

28

The following morning Stone sat down with Marcel, at the latter's request. "We must make a decision, you and I," Marcel said, "about the ownership of Curtis Hall."

"How do you mean?" Stone asked.

"I suggest to you that we might enjoy owning the Curtis property, just the two of us. After all, we are the major investors in the Arrington Group of hotels. We could make it a pet project."

"That is an attractive idea," Stone said, "but I suggest that we form a corporation to own Curtis House, and that you and I own thirty percent each of the shares, and that the remaining forty percent be owned by the Arrington Group, then add a provision that, if the group decides to sell or close the house, you and I will have an opportunity to buy it at a fixed price. That will give us the full support services of the Group, while retaining control of the hotel, but it will also reduce our cash input, something that would make me more comfortable."

"I like your suggestion," Marcel replied. "It achieves all our goals with less money."

"I'll call Woodman & Weld in London and have them write the sales agreement."

"And I will call our bankers and have them produce a bank check for the deposit on the property. You and I should now arrange to move fifteen million pounds each into the Arrington Group's account, to cover the purchase and the renovation."

"Agreed," Stone said, and they each made the necessary phone calls to instruct their bankers. Later in the day the contract was faxed for Stone's approval, and a messenger arrived with the bank check. Stone and Marcel went to Curtis House for drinks, first signing the sales contract with Lady Curtis and handing over the check for the deposit. They finished a little drunk but all very happy.

The electrician began work on the rewiring of the new offices at Windward Hall, following plans specced by Susan overnight, and the following day a team of four painters arrived and began their work. The day after they finished, basic office furniture and computers arrived and were installed, and

Peter and Ben's office manager arrived from Los Angeles to set up the computers and their software, then living in a Windward Hall guest room.

It was two days after the contract signing that the first black SUV, a Mercedes, was seen near the front gates of Windward Hall. Stone called Deputy Chief Inspector Holmes and related the events of the past couple of weeks.

Holmes listened, then spoke: "Has this vehicle trespassed on the property of either Windward Hall or Curtis House?" he asked.

"Not yet," Stone replied.

"Do you have evidence that the occupants of the vehicle possess firearms or have the intention of harming anyone on either estate?"

"No."

"Then I have no cause that would support an arrest. I will, however, cause police cars to drive past the properties twice a day on their regular rounds, and, perhaps, speak to the occupants of the vehicle in a polite fashion, just to let them know we are aware of their presence."

"I think that is a sensible way to proceed," Stone said, "and I thank you for your assistance."

By the beginning of the following week,

Peter, Ben, and their staff of one were in their new offices, and Stone took possession of a small room there, and Susan Blackburn, who was now operating her business from Windward Hall, possessed three rooms. Suitcases of her clothes arrived and were unpacked in the woman's dressing room in the master suite.

Stone had established communications from the house with Woodman & Weld and his major clients. Those phoning the New York office could be connected directly from the firm's switchboard to either Stone's new office or his cell phone, avoiding transatlantic call charges for the callers.

Viv Bacchetti, who had been living quietly, reading a lot, but joining the others for lunch and dinner each day, announced that Strategic Services would require her presence in New York in another week, and that Dino had found a European Union conference on terrorism in Southampton that would require his presence in England for a few days. As part of her work, she conducted a security survey of Curtis House and made recommendations for the installation of equipment and the assignment of personnel to guard the place during the renovation. A Strategic Services aircraft dropped Dino off on the Windward airfield, jet-lagged and a little crabby. The gang received him in the library for cocktails on his first day, and his mood improved exponentially with each Scotch.

Viv gave Dino a tour of the house, and he was much impressed. "I am surprised," he said to Stone, "how much at home here you seem already. The place seems to suit you."

"Suit me it does," Stone said.

"I understand Dr. Don is in the country. Have you had him to tea yet?"

"Not yet, nor for the foreseeable future. He does have one of his black SUVs stationed near our main gate, though, so he hasn't forgotten about us."

"Peter, Ben," Dino said, "tell us how *Hell's Bells* is doing in the States."

"We took in seventy million dollars in sales the first week," Ben replied, "and half again the second week, with eight hundred more screens showing the film. That figure held for the third week, so we have a major hit on our hands. We have a proper London premiere next week at a Leicester Square movie palace. Our stars are coming, and Centurion Studios has taken suites at the Savoy to house them and for interview purposes. We have a premiere in Paris the following weekend."

"I hope you'll stay in the Paris house when

you're there," Stone said. "Maybe you'll think of a story that can be shot in Paris."

"What a good idea," Peter said.

Elsie came into the library and bent close to Stone's ear. "There's a phone call for you, Mr. Barrington," she said, "from a person called" — she referred to a note in her hand — "Dr. Don Beverly Calhoun."

29

Stone took the call in a far corner of the library. "Yes?"

"Mr. Barrington, this is Dr. Don Beverly Calhoun. I think you know who I am."

"Oh, yes, I know who you are."

"I thought that, since we have similar interests, perhaps we should meet and have a chat."

"Similar interests? You and I?"

"We are both interested in Curtis House and in your son and his partner."

"Mr. Calhoun —" Stone said.

"That's Dr. Calhoun."

"Oh, yes, you hold a Ph.D. from that South Carolina diploma mill, don't you?"

"Mr. Barrington —"

"*Mr.* Calhoun, you have no legitimate interest in either of the subjects you just mentioned, particularly the latter one, and I would advise you, most seriously, to back away from both."

"Or suffer the consequences? Do I detect a threat in your words?"

"I make it a point not to make threats, except in a legal context."

"Then let's get legal: I am contemplating suing your son and his partner for libel."

"In Britain?"

"Possibly."

"Then I suggest you ask your attorneys to advise you on the perils of proving libel here. It is more difficult than, perhaps, you have read in the newspapers, and it is *very* expensive. It's even more difficult in the United States."

"I have the resources to press such a suit to its conclusion," Calhoun said.

"And my son has not only his resources, but mine to back him up, plus those of a major Hollywood film studio. Such an ill-considered action would have the eventual effect of reducing your financial status to a smoking ruin."

"I'm told I have grounds, in either country."

"Then you are poorly advised. Have you even seen the film?"

"I have."

"And you still believe the nonsense you have been told?"

"It is not nonsense."

"I should tell you that the film has been reviewed by the best legal counsel in both countries, and they did not find it necessary to make a single cut in order to defend it. But if you wish to squander the fortune you have sucked from the pockets of your credulous followers, then do what you must."

"Now, now, Mr. Barrington, don't you think that in a friendly chat we could iron out our differences?"

"On what basis?"

"For a start, I am willing to pay you a million pounds more than you have agreed to pay for Curtis House. How does that sound? A quick million-pound profit in less than a week?"

"I would not consider it a good return on investment to have you and your followers for neighbors."

"Must we descend into telephone insults?"

"Certainly, I would prefer to insult you to your face, but since I have no intention of meeting you, the phone will have to do."

"I warn you, Mr. Barrington, I am keeping abreast of your movements and actions."

"And how did that work out for you in the states of Connecticut and New York? I should tell you that the law in this country with regard to firearms is much stricter than in the States, and I should also tell you that you have already attracted the attention of local law enforcement, and that private security arrangements for my property are in place. Now, since we have nothing further to discuss, I bid you good day." Stone hung up.

Peter got up and walked over to where Stone sat. "Is everything all right, Dad?"

"Did you overhear my end of the conversation?"

"Well, toward the end you were sort of shouting."

"I apologize, but I was speaking to Dr. Don Beverly Calhoun."

"Ah, I see."

"He's threatening a libel suit, but don't be concerned. You should, however, call the studio and have them call your British distributors and warn them. If he proceeds, Calhoun will ask for an injunction to stop distribution, pending disposition of his suit, and if they aren't ready, he might get it, at least temporarily. British businesspeople get very skittish at the mention of libel, because the laws are so different here. I should think that a little proactive PR defense would be a good idea. You should give a couple of interviews and address the problem head-on. Say that your legal advisers have told you there are no grounds for such a suit."

"They have already done so, and they didn't ask for a single cut."

"I thought as much." Stone picked up the phone. "Excuse me for a moment, I have another call to make." Peter went back to his seat, and Stone called Felicity Devonshire.

"Yes, my dear?"

"I have just had a phone conversation with Dr. Don Beverly Calhoun."

"And how did that go?"

Stone related the substance of the conversation. "Could you speak to the Home Secretary again?"

"Give me more ammo."

"Calhoun's people followed me in Connecticut and New York and were arrested for carrying illegal firearms. As we speak, one of his trademark SUVs is parked near my front gate, and I have alerted the local authorities. I think that indicates a disregard for the law in three places, not to mention the fact that the man is a suspect in the murder of a journalist in California who had the temerity to tell the truth about him."

"I'll see what I can do."

"You are a sweetheart."

"Of course I am." She hung up.

Stone rejoined the others.

"Has your blood pressure returned to normal yet?" Peter asked.

"Almost."

"Another Knob Creek?"

"What a good idea."

"What did Felicity say?"

"Was I shouting again?"

"No, but in the circumstances, she seemed the next logical call."

"You are such a smart young man — it must be an inherited trait."

"Yes, Mom was very smart."

30

Stone, Dino, and Marcel took a morning ride around the Curtis estate the following morning.

"I am very impressed with the beauty of the place," Marcel said. "That should be a great added attraction for guests."

"There's also the river," Stone pointed out. "The staff could conduct wildlife tours by boat, and sailing on the Solent could be offered."

"What about that?" Dino asked, pointing. "Is that an added attraction?" He was pointing at the black Mercedes SUV that had been parked on the main road. It was now moving slowly around the property, not bothering to stick to the drive.

"No," Stone said, "that is trespassing." He got out his phone, called Deputy Chief Inspector Holmes, and reported the intrusion, then hung up. "He's sending a car," Stone said. "In the meantime, ignore them."

They rode on at a walk, and the car continued its tour. After about ten minutes, a police car showed up, its blue light flashing. They stopped the SUV, and the two officers got out and had a look inside. Four men got out of the vehicle and were searched, and each was relieved of a black pistol, all four of which were put into the police car by one of the officers, while the other used a radio.

"This is wonderful news," Stone said. "The stupid bastards were armed."

Shortly a police van arrived and transported the arrestees off the property, followed by the police car and the SUV, now driven by an officer. Stone and his party watched all this from a distance of about a hundred yards, then continued their ride.

Back at the house for lunch, Stone called Felicity Devonshire. "I have more ammo," he said.

"Oh, tell me, please, I'm seeing the Home Secretary this afternoon."

"Four of Dr. Don's people were arrested this morning, after they drove their SUV onto the Curtis estate. They were all armed with handguns, and the police took them away."

"Can you connect them to Dr. Don?"

"You'll have to ask Deputy Chief Inspector Holmes about that, but in my experience, Dr. Don's people carry business cards."

"I will look into that immediately. Thank you, my dear." She hung up.

Stone had just finished lunch when Felicity called back. "Good news," she said, "the four trespassers were, indeed, carrying business cards, connecting them to Dr. Don. They are being transported to New Scotland Yard as we speak and will have a hearing tomorrow morning, at which my service and the Home Secretary will be in attendance."

"What is the likely outcome of the hearing?"

"They might be offered the opportunity to accept immediate expulsion from Britain, or they could be bound over for trial. There will probably be some negotiation with their solicitors over this."

"Will they go after Dr. Don, as well?"

"He would deny having ordered them to be armed, so it's unlikely a judge would expel him. This incident will, however, weigh with the Home Secretary in his deliberations. I'll call you tomorrow and let you know how it comes out."

"Do you think I could attend the hearing?"

"It's open to the public." She gave him the address.

"Wonderful." They hung up, and Stone went to find Dino and tell him what was happening.

"I'll go with you, if that's okay," Dino said.

Stone then got a call from the public prosecutor who was acting for the government at the hearing, and he asked Stone many questions about Dr. Don and the Chosen Few.

"My name is Derek Aslett," he said. "Felicity Devonshire tells me you are attending the hearing tomorrow morning."

"That's correct."

"Would you be good enough to testify to the facts you have just told me and to your experience with the Chosen Few?"

"I would be very happy to testify."

"Please be at the court at a quarter to ten tomorrow morning, then. Do you have the address?"

"I do. May I have your phone and fax numbers?"

Aslett gave them to him. "I will find you in the public gallery." They said goodbye and hung up.

"I'm going to get a shot at Dr. Don at the

hearing," Stone said to Dino.

"I'm going to enjoy watching that," Dino replied.

"Would you call the director of the FBI and get his permission to show Dr. Don's file to the prosecutor? I can fax it to him."

"Sure."

"We'll have to leave here about seven o'clock in the morning," Stone said, "because of the rush-hour traffic."

"That's okay. I'm accustomed to earlier hours than you."

Dino called the director and got permission to use the file, and Stone faxed it to Derek Aslett.

31

Stone and Dino arrived at the court at 9:30 and were allowed into the courtroom. It didn't have the paneling and atmosphere of the Old Bailey it was more modern and plainer. They took a seat, and chatted idly for a few minutes as a few people wandered in and sat down. The prosecutor turned up shortly and introduced himself. "Thank you for the FBI file," he said to Stone. "That has already been very helpful, as I was able to get a search warrant for Calhoun's rooms."

"Great."

"I will first establish the circumstances of the arrest of the four defendants, then I will call you to help establish the character of Calhoun and his organization. Felicity has been helpful in giving me some background on you. Commissioner Bacchetti, I've been told of your background, as well, and I would like, perhaps, to call you for testimony on the file, depending on how things go."

"I'm happy to help if I can," Dino said.

The defendants were brought up from below stairs and sat down in the dock. Stone realized he had seen two of them before, and he told the prosecutor. Then he saw Dr. Don Beverly Calhoun come into the courtroom with a woman and two other men.

Aslett began by calling the arresting officer and walking him through his actions.

"Did the defendants possess firearms?"

"Yes, each of them was armed with a loaded Glock semiautomatic pistol."

"Did they carry identification documents?"

"Yes, each of them carried an American passport, a driver's license, and a business card identifying him as a public relations officer for an organization called the Chosen Few."

"Did you arrest them in the act of trespass on private property?"

"I did."

The man was excused, and Stone was called and sworn.

"Please state your name for the record," Aslett said.

"Stone Barrington."

"You are an American?"

"I am."

"What is your profession?"

"I am an attorney-at-law licensed in the state of New York. I also serve on a number of corporate boards, and I am an investor in some of them."

"Did you recently purchase a property in Hampshire?"

"I did."

"What is its name?"

"Windward Hall."

"Did you, this week, purchase a neighboring property?"

"I did. I have signed a contract to purchase, and the completion will take place soon."

"Its name?"

"Curtis House."

"Are you the sole owner of these properties?"

"I am the sole owner of Windward Hall. I have two partners in Curtis House, an individual and a hotel corporation."

"When you made the offer to purchase Curtis House, were you aware that there was another offer pending?"

"I was."

"Were you aware of the identity of the other bidder?"

"I was. It was a man called Calhoun."

"Is he present in the courtroom, and if so, will you point him out?"

"He is, seated at the rear of the courtroom." Stone pointed to him and got a scowl in return.

"Had you had some previous experience with Dr. Calhoun or his associates?"

"Yes, I had driven from New York to a town in the neighboring state of Connecticut, and one of his associates followed me there. Calhoun wrongly believes that a film made by my son is intended as an unfavorable depiction of him. The person who followed me is one of the defendants, the one on the right." He pointed. "He told the front desk at the inn where I was lunching that he wanted to see my son, who was not present in Connecticut. I confronted him, there was a scuffle, and I took a nine-millimeter Glock from him. Later, he continued to follow me, and I reported this to the Connecticut State Police, who disarmed him and arrested him for carrying a firearm without a license. He also had a loaded shotgun in his car."

"Did you have any further contact with associates of Dr. Calhoun?"

"Yes. When I drove back to New York the following day I began being followed as I crossed the New York State line. I called the police, and they disarmed and arrested him. He is the defendant on the left, and he was also carrying a Glock and a shotgun in his car."

"Did you have any further contact with associates of Dr. Calhoun?"

"Not in New York, not until I flew to England a few days later."

Aslett picked up the FBI file. "Prior to your departure, did you come to learn more about Dr. Calhoun and his associates?"

"Yes."

"I show you a file from the American Federal Bureau of Investigation, which is analogous to our MI5. Did you come to read this?"

"Yes."

"And what did you learn of Dr. Calhoun and his organization, the Chosen Few?"

"I learned that it was a religious cult centered on Calhoun, and that his organization was a suspect in the murder of a journalist who had written an uncomplimentary article about them."

Another lawyer in the room rose. "Objection to the characterization of the Chosen Few as a cult. It is a respected religious organization in the United States."

"Respected by whom?" Stone asked.

"Mr. Barrington," the judge said, "you will not question members of the court."

"I apologize, Your Lordship."

"When did you next encounter Dr. Calhoun or members of his cult?" Aslett asked.

"When I returned to England a neighbor told me that Calhoun had made an offer on the property next door, and that he had been looking for such a property for several weeks."

"And subsequent to that you made an offer for the property that was accepted?"

"Yes."

"Did you then begin to have contact with associates of Dr. Calhoun?"

"Yes. I discovered that a strange vehicle was parked near my front gate, and I notified the police. Subsequent to that, I had a telephone call from Calhoun, offering to buy the Curtis property from me, which I refused. During this call Calhoun threatened to sue my son and his associates in the production of his film for libel. I declined his offer. It was later that day that I saw the Calhoun vehicle on the Curtis property and I called the police again."

"And that brings us to the present moment," Aslett said. "No further questions, Mr. Barrington. You are excused."

Stone got down from the stand and took

his seat.

A police officer came into the courtroom and whispered something to Aslett.

"Does the prosecution have any other witnesses?" the judge asked.

"One, Your Honor, a police officer."

A uniformed officer was sworn in and identified himself as Inspector Marshall.

"Inspector Marshall, did you this morning obtain a warrant to search the hotel rooms occupied by Dr. Don Beverly Calhoun and his associates?"

"Yes, sir, I did."

"And did you conduct the search?"

"I did, sir."

"Did you find anything illegal in these rooms?"

"Yes, sir. We found three Glock handguns."

The defense lawyer stood and looked at Calhoun, who nodded to him. "Your Lordship, we request a brief recess in these proceedings in order to confer with the prosecution."

The judge looked up at the courtroom clock. "We will adjourn for lunch and return at one o'clock. The defendants will be returned to their cells, and Dr. Calhoun and his associates will not leave the courtroom, unless accompanied by a police officer."

Stone and Dino adjourned to a nearby pub for lunch.

32

Stone and Dino were back in the courtroom shortly before one o'clock, and at the stroke of the hour Derek Aslett returned and sat down. The four defendants did not appear in the dock. Everyone rose as the judge entered and called the court to order.

"Mr. Aslett, how do you wish to proceed at this time?"

"Your Lordship, during the lunch hour I met with counsel for the defense, and we have agreed, with the approval of the court, on a plea of guilty to one charge each of criminal trespass and possession of an illegal firearm by the four defendants. Additionally, they will each pay a fine of one thousand pounds. Dr. Calhoun, his wife, and two companions will plead guilty to one count each of possession of an illegal firearm and a fine of one thousand pounds, on the condition that all of them be permitted to pack their bags and pay their hotel bills, then be escorted to Heathrow Airport, where they will leave the country on the first available flight to New York, and that they not return to the United Kingdom at any time in the future."

"Does the defense agree to these pleas and these terms?" the judge asked.

The defense counsel rose. "Your Lordship, the defense concurs."

"Very well, the police will transport the eight of them to their respective hotels, where they will pack their bags and pay their bills. The defendants will also pay their fines in pounds sterling or United States dollars, then be transported to Heathrow, where the police will see them aboard the first available flight to New York. They will be barred from returning to the United Kingdom, without the written permission of the Home Secretary." He banged his gavel, everyone rose, and he left the courtroom.

Aslett walked over to where Stone and Dino stood. "I hope you find that a satisfactory outcome," he said, beaming.

"I would have preferred seeing them sent to the Tower of London and beheaded," Stone said, "but short of that, I'll settle for your deal."

"Commissioner, I'm glad we did not have to call you."

"So am I," Dino replied.

"By the way, today's flights are all full, so I've booked them in steerage on a British Airways flight out of Heathrow at ten AM tomorrow, and they'll have the pleasure of spending a night in the departure area, without access to the first-class lounge or the Concorde Room."

"Good move," Stone said. They shook hands with him and left the courtroom.

Outside, they paused to watch, with satisfaction, as Calhoun and his cohorts were loaded into a Black Maria and driven away.

"And good riddance," Stone said as the van departed.

"I had a thought," Dino said.

"Tell me."

"The judge ordered them to pay their fines in cash, so Aslett must have been told by their lawyer that they have it available."

"That makes sense."

"I'm acquainted with the head of customs at Kennedy. Why don't I give him a call and suggest that Calhoun and his crowd be checked for excess cash when they land? They're only allowed to carry five thousand dollars in or out of the country, unless they declare it to customs. If they don't, they're subject to federal prosecution."

"Dino, I love the way your mind works,"

Stone said.

They got back into Stone's car and drove toward the motorway south, while Dino made the call on his cell phone.

Stone's phone rang, and he used the hands-free feature of the car's sound system to answer it. "Hello?"

"Stone, it's Julian Whately. I met with Lady Curtis's solicitor this morning and we worked through the closing documents and made any necessary changes. They're ready for yours, M'sieur duBois's, and Lady Curtis's signatures. I'm told that she has already moved her things out of the house and is staying temporarily with Dame Felicity Devonshire. She has said she is available for completion at ten o'clock tomorrow morning."

"That was fast, Julian."

"We do what we can."

"Please overnight everything to me, and would you please call Lady Curtis or her solicitor and ask if we might meet at ten tomorrow at Windward Hall for the completion?"

"Of course. The package is on its way."

They hung up, and a moment later Stone's phone rang again. "Hello?"

"It's Felicity."

"Hello, there."

"I've just heard of the outcome of this morning's proceedings. You must be very pleased."

"I certainly am."

"I'm pleased, too, and so is the Home Secretary, because he won't have to go to the bother of kicking Dr. Don out of the country and dealing with his appeal."

"The judge also said they can't come back here without the Home Secretary's written permission."

"Which, in the circumstances, neither he nor his possible successors will ever give."

He told her about the travel arrangements Aslett had made for the group and got a big laugh from her. "Dino has also arranged for U.S. Customs to search them for excess cash on their arrival," Stone said.

"Oh, good! I don't think Dr. Don is ever going to mess you about again."

"Not in England, anyway. Oh, by the way, I've just heard that Glynnis Curtis has moved out of her house and is staying with you. We're planning to complete the sale at Windward Hall tomorrow morning."

"Funny how fast everything moves when everyone involved wants it to. I hear Susan is already at work on making Curtis House into the next Arrington."

"She is."

"Aren't you glad you took my suggestion about seeing her socially?"

"It's all worked out very well."

"I promise not to tread on her turf, so to speak, but you'll be free again soon enough — you always are."

"I hardly know how to respond to that."

"Perhaps I'll have the Muddle East sorted out enough to come down for the weekend, and we can all have dinner."

"Wonderful idea, and we'll do it at Windward Hall."

"I look forward to that." She hung up.

"Your luck is holding out, isn't it?" Dino said.

"Let's hope it continues," Stone replied.

33

Dr. Don Beverly Calhoun stepped down from the Black Maria at Heathrow, took his wife's hand, and followed two uniformed police officers through immigration and security; then they were led to a departure gate lounge, where two other officers met them.

"Your flight leaves at ten o'clock tomorrow morning," an officer said to them. "So make yourselves as comfortable as you can."

"Why can't we go to an airport hotel?" Calhoun asked indignantly. "We'll hardly be comfortable here."

"A restaurant is over there, restrooms are in that direction, newspapers and magazines, too," the officer said.

"We'd like to go to the first-class lounge, then," Calhoun said.

"You don't have first-class tickets, so that's not possible."

"I have a credit card that will get us inside."

"Denied," the officer said firmly, and walked away.

Calhoun's wife, who was twenty-five years younger than he, pitched a fit. "I can't live like this!" she screamed.

"You can and will until we're in New York," he said firmly, but that did not quiet her. She bitched until the night had passed and they had boarded their flight to Kennedy, and then she bitched about being in tourist class.

By the time they had arrived in New York, Calhoun was, himself, feeling very much as she did. They cleared immigration and were headed through customs when they were redirected to a special counter, where four officers awaited them.

"Open everything," their supervisor said to Calhoun, while taking his large briefcase from him, placing it on a counter, and opening it. "Ah, what do we have here?" he asked, viewing the stacks of hundred-dollar bills and fifty-pound notes.

"There's no law against carrying cash," Calhoun replied.

"Let me see your declaration form for the cash."

"What?"

"You're allowed to bring only five thousand dollars into the country without a declaration."

"But I took it out with me."

"You were supposed to file a declaration then, too. That's two offenses."

Other officers were discovering cash in other suitcases.

"You can take five thousand dollars with you," the supervisor said, handing him a stack of hundreds. "We're confiscating the rest, pending a court hearing."

Calhoun sagged. "I hope to God the cars I ordered are waiting," he said to his steaming wife.

They were waiting, he discovered, after an hour and a half in customs, in a distant parking lot. After a long walk, they piled into the cars and were driven to Calhoun's high-rise apartment in Manhattan.

There, with a drink in hand, Calhoun began to think about revenge.

The package containing the closing documents for the sale of Curtis House arrived at Windward Hall early the following morning, and Stone had time to review them before the ten AM completion. He reflected that everything was so much simpler when a mortgage company was not a party to the sale.

Lady Curtis looked somehow younger than the last time he had seen her. He assumed it was because a load had been lifted from her shoulders, and she was now independently wealthy, if she had not been before. She signed the documents eagerly, as did Stone and Marcel, and she turned over all the well-tagged keys to the house, then they adjourned for a light lunch.

Afterward, Susan showed Marcel and Stone the computer renditions of the main rooms of Curtis House and the plans were approved with few changes.

"Now I've got to go back to London, put my own house in order, and get work started on the draperies and wallpaper. I've got three crews arriving on Monday morning, one for the public rooms, one for the bedrooms, and one for the bathrooms. The engineering drawings for the new heating and air-conditioning systems will be along in a couple of weeks, and we'll send them out for bids to companies in the area."

"That's good," Marcel said. "Our neighbors will think better of us if we use local outfits, instead of bringing everything down from London."

Stone walked Susan out to her car. "When

will I see you?"

"Next weekend, and after that I'll be working almost entirely from here, getting the plans organized for our application for the planning commission."

"Won't we need an architect for that?"

"I am a licensed architect with a degree from Cambridge," she said.

"I didn't know, but that's very handy."

"Various people will come down from London in aid of restructuring my company, and I'll interview job applicants here, too. Would you prefer it if I worked from Curtis House?"

"Whatever is most convenient for you. I'm happy to have you here, but we've given you all the space we have available, and I'll understand if it's not enough."

"I'll give that some thought and let you know," she said.

He kissed her, and she drove away in her green Range Rover.

"What a package," he said aloud to himself.

34

After Susan had driven away, Stan brought the Land Rover around for Marcel.

"You're leaving so soon?" Stone asked.

"Yes, my airplane is on the way to your field. I must run to Paris, then Rome for a few days, to keep our kettles boiling there, then I'll be back."

"You'll be very welcome," Stone said.

"I've left a few things in my room," Marcel said, "including some laundry."

"I'll see that it's taken care of."

Marcel got into the car and was driven away.

Stone and Dino walked over to the stables, where horses had been saddled for them.

"You should keep some riding clothes here," Stone said.

"What riding clothes? I don't own any."

"There's a shop in Beaulieu that will fix you up."

They mounted, then rode across the

meadow, through the wood, then jumped the stone wall onto the Curtis House property. There were two large moving vans parked in front of the house, and furniture was being loaded on them.

"They're going to London, to Susan's workshop, for reupholstering," Stone explained.

"Susan is quite a girl," Dino said. "Why don't you hang on to her?"

"I'd like that, but I don't know if she's going to have time for me. She's expanding her company while redoing Curtis House, and she's got her hands full."

"She doesn't work nights, does she?"

"That's what's keeping us going."

They rode slowly around the property, seeing things they hadn't noticed before.

"I saw the hermit's house," Dino said. "I'll bet the brigadier was an interesting guy."

"I never met him, and saw him on the property only twice."

"You remember when we were young, back at the Nineteenth, and got our first big homicide?"

"How could I forget?"

"Remember the lesbian lady who offed herself in the bathtub?"

"I do."

"And we thought for a while she had done

it out of guilt, but it turned out she wasn't the murderer?"

"I do."

"Ever since, I've always been suspicious when suicides confess."

"As I recall, she didn't confess."

"Right, but we assumed she was guilty, anyway."

"I see your point. Are you suspicious of the brigadier's confession?"

"Sometimes there are motives for suicide other than guilt," Dino said. "I don't know enough about this one to form an opinion, but I think you ought to keep that in mind."

"Why? I'm not investigating it. I accept his confession as sincere."

"Maybe you ought to know more about the case," Dino said, then spurred his horse into a gallop and jumped another stone wall.

Stone followed him and concentrated on the wall, putting everything else out of his mind.

Dr. Don was enjoying his first breakfast back in New York, and his wife, Cheree, seemed to be, as well. "How are you feeling?" he asked her.

"Well, I hadn't expected to be back in New York this soon. I thought we were going to buy that house and operate over there for a while."

"Well, yes . . ."

"After all, it's gotten a little hot on this side of the Atlantic, hasn't it? I mean, that magazine piece we heard about is going to come out sooner or later. What was it, *New York?*"

"The New Yorker."

"You should never have given that woman the interview."

"Oh, I don't know, at least I got my side of the story told."

"You just wanted to screw her," Cheree said with a snort. "Did you, by the way?"

"I did not, she was not my type."

"Oh, Don, your type is anything with a pussy."

He laughed. "I've been accused of that."

"I thought I was keeping you satisfied."

"Oh, you are, my sweet," he said, patting her on the knee. He finished his coffee just as the doorbell rang, and he went to answer it. He opened the door to find the *New Yorker* writer, Lisa Altman, standing there.

"Good morning," she said brightly.

"How did you get past the doorman?" he asked.

"Oh, we're old friends," she said. "May I come in?"

"Of course," he said, stepping back and

admitting her.

"*The New Yorker* is gearing up to run my profile on you, and I wanted to ask a couple more questions, if you don't mind."

"Sure." He led her into the living room, with its spectacular view of Central Park, and sat her down facing the window. "Now," he said, settling into a chair, "what can I tell you?"

"Tell me how you managed to get yourself declared persona non grata from Britain."

Calhoun was stunned. "How on earth . . . ?"

"Oh, you made the papers this morning. Haven't you seen the *Times*?"

He had not. His secretary didn't know they were back; she hadn't restarted the papers. "No. What did they have to say?"

"Only that you, your wife, and half a dozen of your staff had been hauled into court, charged with trespassing and possession of illegal weapons, and fined and deported."

"Oh, they've blown that all out of proportion. We had an argument over a real estate deal, and the fastest way to settle it was just to leave."

"And not come back?" she asked, while taking notes on a pad.

"That's just temporary."

"What sort of real estate deal?"

"We were looking at a country house and some property. Somebody outbid us."

"And that would be a Mr. Stone Barrington?"

Calhoun blinked. "Ah, yes, he owns an adjoining property."

"And two of your people were arrested earlier in New York and Connecticut on weapons charges, weren't they?"

"I'm afraid they hadn't researched the local laws on the subject. They're Westerners, you see, and unaccustomed to restrictions on Second Amendment rights."

"So that's twice you've had to exert your Second Amendment rights against Mr. Barrington? Is there some sort of animus between you?"

"Certainly not on my part," Calhoun said, sounding wounded. "His son has made a defamatory film about me."

"Oh, yes, *Hell's Bells.* Nice title."

"We'll be filing a libel suit soon."

"Libel is tough to prove. Are you sure you have enough evidence? Movie scripts are very well vetted by the studios before they're put into production."

"I don't want to say too much at this point." He looked at his watch. "Goodness, I have an appointment. You're going to have to excuse me," he said, rising. "Let me show you out."

He got her out the door, then went back to the kitchen. "That *New Yorker* woman is back," he said. "She says they're running her profile soon."

"Maybe we'd better go back to L.A.," she said.

"Not just yet," he replied. "I've some work to do here." He picked up the phone and dialed a number.

35

The following morning, early, Stone got a phone call from Joan. "You didn't tell me you were redecorating the house," she said.

"How's that again?"

"The paint job on the front of the house. Did you order that done?"

"No, I didn't. What kind of a paint job?"

"Pink," she said, "with dirty words. I shouldn't have to read them to you, they're always on the tip of your tongue."

"Any messages?"

"Something about Second Amendment rights."

"Take pictures, e-mail them to Dino and me, then call the police and say we suspect followers of Dr. Don Beverly Calhoun. He arrived in New York yesterday. I don't know if he's in a hotel or home in California. Then get somebody to come in and clean the facade. They may have to clean it all the

226

way to the top to get a match in the brick color."

"Okay. Anything else?"

"Yes, call Mike Freeman and ask him to put an armed guard in your reception area, so he can see out the window. Twenty-four/seven, until further notice."

"I'll feel so safe," she said. "I hope he's cute."

"Don't distract him." Stone hung up and called Dino's room and told him what had happened. "You'll have the photos in a minute."

"What do you need?"

"I need to make Dr. Don's life continuously miserable until he crawls back into his hole."

"Sounds like that's what he's trying to do to you."

"Right. I want to trump him."

"Does he have a residence in New York?"

"I don't know."

"I'll look into that. The New York State tax department is on a tear about part-time residents right now. They seem to think that anybody who breathes in New York should pay income taxes."

"What a good idea!"

"Oh, by the way, I got a call: U.S. Customs nailed Dr. Don at Kennedy with something over a hundred thousand bucks and half that much in pounds, confiscated it all, except five thousand dollars, pending a hearing."

"Oh, grand! See you later."

Stone's bedside phone rang. "Hello?"

"Mr. Barrington, my name is Lisa Altman. I'm a writer for *The New Yorker.*"

"Good morning, how can I help you?"

"We're about to publish a profile of Dr. Don Beverly Calhoun."

"I'm delighted to hear it. I'm sure he won't like it."

"I'm sure, too. I spoke to Dr. Don yesterday and asked him why he is now persona non grata in the U.K. He said it was over a real estate argument with you."

"Have you got a tape recorder running?"

"I will in two seconds . . . there."

Stone gave her an account of events since Peter's movie opened, right up to having his New York house repainted.

"Sounds like war," she said.

"Does Calhoun have an apartment in New York?"

"Yes, on West Fifty-seventh Street, high up in one of those skinny, impossibly expensive buildings." She gave him the street and apartment number.

"Do you know how long he's had it?"

"Since the building opened last year, and he had another place on Central Park West before that." She gave him the address.

"For how long?"

"Something like ten years, I believe."

"I hope you'll include the painting of my house in your piece," Stone said. "I can e-mail you fresh photos."

"Thank you, I'd like to see them."

"Other news: I've just heard that Calhoun was searched in customs at Kennedy yesterday, and they found a hundred grand in dollars and fifty grand in pounds, all confiscated, except the legal five thousand dollars, pending a hearing. And that's after he paid eight thousand pounds in cash fines before departing London."

"I'll call customs right away and get a quote."

Stone had a thought. "How close are you to publishing?"

"Next week."

"Could you delay it for a week in order to peruse a file on Calhoun from a certain federal law enforcement agency? One that could be anonymously delivered to you today, and the source of which will never be revealed? The Brits saw it before Calhoun's deportation."

"I'll know as soon as I see it."

"Within the hour," Stone said, grabbing a pencil. "Where are you?"

"At the *New Yorker* building." She gave him a room number.

"Bye." He hung up and called Joan. "Please send the FBI file on Calhoun, in a plain brown wrapper, no return address, to the following person." He read her the name and address. "Include prints of your architectural photos." He hung up and called Dino. "Here's Dr. Don's address in New York. He's lived there for a year. Before that he lived at this address on Central Park West."

Dino wrote them down. "You've been busy."

"Not busy, lucky. I'll tell you over lunch."

36

Two days later, Dr. Don received a letter from the New York State tax people, demanding his federal tax returns for the past four years and a list of the days he had spent in New York during those years and their purpose. He immediately called his accountant. "How the hell am I supposed to get all this information?"

"I have your tax returns. Do you have a diary or keep a calendar of your travels?"

"Yes."

"Then extract the information they want and send it to me. I'll send them a letter saying that we're working on it."

"Are they going to hit me for back taxes?"

"It's too early to tell. Do you pay state taxes in California?"

"No."

"Where is your legal residence?"

"In Florida."

"For how long?"

"Four years."

"Where was your legal residence before that?"

"I'm not sure, exactly."

"You don't know where you lived four years ago?"

"Maybe New Mexico, maybe Georgia."

"Did you pay state taxes in either of those?"

"Yes, in Georgia."

"Send me the info, and I'll get started."

"How long is it going to take to clear this up?"

"Many months, maybe years."

"Oh, shit."

"That's what everybody says." He hung up.

Less than an hour later, Dr. Don received another call.

"Good morning, it's Lisa, at *The New Yorker.*"

He managed a smiling voice. "Good morning, Lisa."

"I've received an anonymous tip that the New York State tax authorities are investigating you. Any truth to that?"

"Are you in cahoots with my mailman? I just got a letter an hour ago."

"Like I said, the source is anonymous —

sounds accurate, though. What did they ask you for?"

"Tax returns, my schedule in New York."

"Uh-oh."

"That's pretty much what my accountant said, though in a great many more billable words."

"Thanks, that's all I needed to know. Oh, just one more thing: Why did you paint the front of Stone Barrington's house?"

"I have no idea what you're talking about. Goodbye, Lisa." He hung up.

"Now what?" his wife asked.

"We're down a point," Calhoun replied.

Stone and Dino were about to leave for their morning ride when Lady Bourne, née Elizabeth Bowen, pulled up in her car and got out.

"Good morning, Elizabeth," Stone said, shaking her hand and introducing Dino. "How are you?"

"I'm very well, but Charles, I fear, is not."

"I'm sorry to hear that. I thought, perhaps, he looked slimmer on his return from Paris."

"Yes, he's losing weight steadily, not eating well. The doctor comes every day. He thinks we're near the end."

"May I come and see him?"

"I don't think you would enjoy the experience, and he might not even know you're there. I'll give him your regards, and if he asks for you, I'll call."

"Please do."

"I'll tell him you're exercising the horses, too — he'll like that."

"It's more the other way around."

"I want to thank you again for the wonderful honeymoon you gave us in Paris."

"I only gave you the house — you supplied everything else."

"Well, yes, but our visit was greatly enhanced by the house."

"I'm glad."

"By the way, that Inspector Holmes has called twice at the cottage to see Charles, but I sent him away both times. He may come and see you."

"Do you know what it's about?"

"The only contact that Charles has had with the police for many years was over the murder of Richard Curtis by the brigadier. I should think it's in regard to that."

"I see."

"I just thought you should know Holmes might call."

"Thank you."

They shook hands again, and she drove away.

"I wonder what's stirred up the inspector?" Dino asked.

"Who knows?" They mounted their horses and rode away.

37

Dr. Don Beverly Calhoun was having lunch with his wife when the doorman called up. "Dr. Calhoun?"

"Yes?"

"There are two gentlemen at the front desk who have identified themselves as police officers. Shall I send them up?"

"What do they want?"

"They wouldn't tell me, sir, but they showed me badges and IDs."

Calhoun signed. "All right, send them up." He threw down his napkin.

"Now what?" Cheree asked.

"Now there are policemen at the door."

"I've seen enough policemen this week to last me a lifetime," she said.

Dr. Don answered the door and two men showed him badges that were different from each other and insisted he read their IDs.

"All right," Calhoun said, "you're policemen. Now what?"

"May we come in, sir? We'd like to ask you some questions."

"Oh, all right." He took them into the living room and seated them facing away from the view. They didn't deserve it. "What can I do for you?"

"First, I should say that I am Lieutenant Shaw, from the Connecticut State Police, and this is Lieutenant Roberts, from the New York State Police. For your convenience, we are conducting this interview together, rather than separately."

"I derived that from your IDs."

The officer showed him two photographs. "Are these two men your employees?"

"They are employed by a corporate entity of which I am an officer."

"They were arrested, one in Connecticut, one in New York State, and they were both carrying firearms unlicensed in either state."

"I heard about that. I wish to apologize."

"I'm afraid, sir, that apologies do not erase felony arrests. Were they armed on your instructions?"

Calhoun blinked rapidly. "I do not recall giving them such instructions."

"We understand that you and these two men were recently arrested in the United Kingdom on the same charge. Is this correct?"

"That was over a real estate dispute, nothing important."

"Sir, please answer the question."

"Should I have my attorney present?"

"You are not under arrest, sir, but that's entirely up to you."

"How does the business in London relate to the business in Connecticut and New York?"

"It seems to indicate a pattern of behavior, sir."

"I think it would be best if I decline to answer other questions and refer you to my attorney."

"As you wish, sir."

Calhoun wrote down the name and phone number and handed it to them.

"One other question, sir: Do you possess a firearm at this residence?"

"You can ask my attorney that."

"Thank you, sir." The two men rose and headed for the door, then one of them turned back. "I almost forgot," he said, handing Calhoun a blue envelope. "You've been served."

Calhoun was left staring at the envelope as the door closed behind him.

"Served what?" Cheree asked.

Calhoun ripped open the envelope. "Notices to appear in court in both Litchfield,

Connecticut, and Katonah, New York."

"When?"

"Tomorrow. Katonah in the morning, Litchfield in the afternoon."

"Oh, good," she said acidly. "We'll have a nice day in the country."

Calhoun called his attorney and reported his conversation with the two policemen.

"And you said they were your employees?"

"I said I was an officer of the company that employs them. Will you be at this hearing?"

"I'm licensed in both New York and Connecticut. I'll go with you. And I'll bring a couple of blank checks on the firm for bail money."

"Bail money?"

"It's what you pay to get out of jail, like in Monopoly."

"Jail?"

"Dr. Calhoun, if you sent two armed men on some sort of mission, without the requisite firearms licenses, it is very likely that both they and you will be charged."

"Oh, dear Jesus," Calhoun breathed.

"Speak to him, it might help."

38

Stone was in the library, reading some correspondence sent to him by Joan, when Geoffrey appeared. "Excuse me, Mr. Barrington, but Deputy Inspector Holmes is here and wishes to see you."

"All right, Geoffrey, send him in." He rose to greet the policeman, whose demeanor was, as always, neutral. Stone waved him to a seat. "How can I help you, Inspector?"

"Mr. Barrington, during your time at Windward Hall have you become aware of Sir Charles's, ah, family situation?"

"In what respect?"

"In respect to the parentage of his children."

"Ah." Stone thought about it for a moment and decided to tell what he knew; this man was not going to let go. "I have become aware of that," he said.

Holmes produced a notebook. "May I ask how you learned of it?"

"I suppose you could say, from the horse's mouth."

"Could you be explicit about which horse?"

"It was the Sunday night when Sir Charles gave a large party, at which he announced his imminent marriage to the former Elizabeth Bowen. I was sitting on that sofa" — he pointed to the one facing the fire — "and Sir Charles entered the room with another man, who turned out to be his son."

"Leslie?"

"If you say so. I was sort of scrunched down on the sofa, having a brandy, so they couldn't see me, and they spoke freely."

"And what did they have to say?"

"Let's see: the son complained about his father's selling the house to me, instead of keeping it in the family, which I took to mean leaving it to him, or perhaps his sister, or both."

"And how did Sir Charles respond to that?"

"He said that the son's mother had left both her children very well fixed, and he saw no need to enrich them further. Do you know if that is correct?"

"If I may be indiscreet, I believe it is widely thought in the county that most, if not all, of the family money derived from the parentage of the wife, and that their relationship was based at least as much on economics as on familial affection."

"I see. Well, the conversation — or at least, Sir Charles — continued as he explained his son's parentage to him."

"Now we're getting somewhere," Holmes said, displaying unusual relish, for him. "How did he explain it?"

"It went back to an accident many years ago when they were sailing with a group of friends on Sir Charles's yacht. The boy — Leslie, you say?"

"Yes."

"The boy had an accident in which he was cut and bleeding very badly. They got him to a local hospital, but he needed a blood transfusion. Apparently neither of the parents had the same blood type as Leslie."

Holmes consulted his notes. "That would be Type A Positive, for both of them," he said.

"Yes, but the boy had a rarer type."

"That would be Type B Negative," Holmes read from his notes. "The rarest, I believe."

"If you say so. The friends were tested and, fortunately, one of the men present had the correct type. A transfusion was given, and the boy recovered."

"You see the contradiction here?" Holmes asked.

"Yes, it would appear that, since neither of the parents had the rare type, the son would have been fathered by another man."

"Quite so. A man with Type B Negative. Did Sir Charles mention the name of the blood donor?"

"No, he did not. I had the impression that he wished to deny his son knowledge of his parentage, perhaps out of spite. He may have had some other reason, of course — I wouldn't know about that."

"These circumstances are terribly interesting," Holmes said mildly.

"I suppose they are, in a gossipy sort of way, but how does that concern the police?"

"As a possible motive for murder."

"Now," Stone said, "you've lost me."

"Well, as investigator to former investigator, if I may, let us suppose that the owner of the Type B Negative on that day was Sir Richard Curtis."

"All right. You're saying that Sir Charles could have murdered him out of outrage that he had fathered a child with Lady Bourne?"

"Yes, I am."

"But the accident and the knowledge of the blood types occurred decades ago, apparently. That would be a very long time to hold a grudge, to keep outrage on the boil, would it not? Especially since Sir Charles and Sir Richard have been presumed by everybody who knows them, that I have met, to have been the best of friends during those decades."

"I'll grant you that."

"And, in any case, you have a confessor to the murder in the person of the brigadier."

"Wilfred Burns, yes. But what would his motive be?"

"I never met the man, only saw him from a distance a couple of times, so I wouldn't know."

"I've been looking into the backgrounds of the principals in this case," the inspector said, "and in going over their military records I have discovered that Sir Richard was not the only man in the neighborhood who had Type B Negative blood."

"Oh?"

"The brigadier was Type B Negative, as well."

"Interesting, but how would that give the brigadier a motive for murder?"

"Guilt, perhaps."

"Guilt? Guilt over what?"

Stone heard a chiming noise, and the inspector withdrew a watch on a chain from his waistcoat and stared at it, apparently appalled at what he saw. "Good heavens," he said, rising, "I'm afraid I am late for a very important appointment. Please excuse me."

He left the room abruptly, closing the door behind him, leaving Stone baffled.

39

Dr. Don Beverly Calhoun sat in a holding cell in Katonah, New York. His companions were not what Calhoun would consider felicitous company and at least one of them smelled very bad. Calhoun had been there for the better part of two hours, and his discomfort had made it seem twice that.

His attention was drawn to the door by the rattling of a key in the lock. "Which one of you is Calhoun?" the jailer asked.

Calhoun's hand shot up. "I am."

"No," said another prisoner, raising his hand, "I am Calhoun."

Calhoun stood up, terrified that the other man, not he, would be set free. "*I* am Calhoun! Check my wallet — it's in an envelope at the front desk."

"Okay, Calhoun, come with me," the jailer said. He pointed to the interloper. "You, siddown and shaddup."

Calhoun followed the jailer down a hall

and to the front desk, where his attorney waited, clutching a brown envelope.

"Okay," the lawyer said, "you're sprung." He handed Calhoun the envelope. "Your personal effects."

Calhoun followed him to the car, where his wife waited in the backseat, and settled himself in the front passenger seat before retrieving his watch, ring, wallet, and other effects from the envelope.

"Do you know how long I've been sitting in this car?" his wife demanded to know.

"Just about as long as I have been sitting in a cell, I expect."

"I'm sorry it took so long," the attorney said, starting the car. "The wheels of justice grind slowly."

"I'm hungry," Cheree said.

"I'm afraid it's a forty-minute drive to Litchfield, and our hearing is in half an hour," the attorney said.

"Swell."

Forty-five minutes later they entered a small courtroom, glared at by judge and prosecutor.

"I apologize for our tardiness, Your Honor," the attorney said, "but we were in another hearing."

"Let's get on with it," the judge said. "Mr.

Prosecutor?"

The hearing was a near duplicate of the one in Katonah, and once again Calhoun found himself in another cell, this time, mercifully, alone. Less than an hour passed before he was released on bail.

Calhoun watched as his wife greedily consumed a good lunch at a local restaurant. It had always annoyed him that she could eat for an hour with both hands and not gain an ounce. He ate just enough to keep his blood sugar up, afraid that he might throw up on the table if he ate more.

Back in the car, Calhoun rounded on his attorney. "How long am I going to be subjected to this kind of punishment?" he demanded.

"I expect for as long as you keep behaving stupidly, Don," the attorney replied, disrespectfully using his first name.

"So you think I myself am to blame for all this?"

"Of course I do."

"That is outrageous."

"I hope you're referring to your conduct," the attorney said. "And while we're on the subject, did you send your minions to paint the facade of Stone Barrington's house?"

Calhoun made sputtering noises.

"I'll take that as confirmation. Have you not yet realized, after three hearings in two countries, that you are trying to intimidate someone who will not be intimidated? Have you behaved in this manner in the other cities in which you live?"

"Certainly not," Calhoun spat.

"Well, let's see: you've been run out of Atlanta, New Orleans, Albuquerque, and Britain so far, and maybe Los Angeles, too."

"I have not been run out of anywhere!" Calhoun shouted. "I simply enjoy experiencing different cities and countries!"

"Have you ever Googled yourself?"

"I don't know how to do that."

"I recommend it for getting a clear picture of your past," the attorney said. "Your bio on Wikipedia makes you sound like a megalomaniacal lunatic."

"Then I'll sue . . . whoever you said that was."

"Then that makes you a hyper-litigious, megalomaniacal lunatic."

"You, sir, are fired as my attorney!" Calhoun screamed.

"And that, sir, is a great relief!" The attorney whipped into a rest stop on the Connecticut–New York border and screeched to a halt. "Get out!"

"What?"

"Get out of my car! You are no longer my client, and I will not devote another minute to chauffeuring you from hearing to hearing! And take that woman with you!" he yelled, jerking a thumb at Cheree.

"Let's go, Don," Cheree said, opening her own door.

The two of them got out, and the attorney drove away, leaving them standing in front of the public restrooms.

Calhoun was slapping his pockets. "Where is my phone?"

She handed it to him. "You gave it to me when they locked you up the first time. Now you get on it and get us a car out of here. I have to pee." She stormed away, leaving him looking for a car service.

40

Stone drove Dino and Viv down to the airstrip, and on the way he told them of his conversation with Deputy Chief Inspector Holmes. "Does that make any sense to you?" he asked them.

"Guilt over what?" Dino asked.

"Before he could answer that question his pocket watch alarm went off, and he fled the premises."

"Well, let me know when you find out," Dino said. They pulled up to the waiting Strategic Services G450, and the crew took their bags from the Bentley and stowed them on the airplane.

"How's the weather for our flight?" Dino asked the pilot.

"Looks very good," the man said. "We'll be in Teterboro by early afternoon."

Stone hugged them both, put them aboard the airplane, watched it take off, then drove back to the main house. He went downstairs to his little office and sat down at his desk. Peter came in.

"How's it going, Dad?"

"Pretty well. I just put Dino and Viv on their plane to New York."

"Good news — we got script and budget approval for our film. The production company is coming down today with a truckload of lights, cameras, and editing equipment. We should start shooting the first of the week in the rooms that Susan is finishing up now."

"Wonderful news." Peter turned to go, and Stone checked his e-mail and called him back. "You might want to see this. It's from Arthur Steele, head of the Steele Group of insurance companies." He turned the monitor so Peter could see it.

Dear Stone, I saw Peter's movie, *Hell's Bells,* last night, and I thought it was wonderful.

"That's nice," Peter said.

"There's more," Stone replied.

I saw the mention of some sort of real estate fraud that the character had going, and coincidentally, a report landed on my desk, calling my attention to the fact that among our household insurance accounts, it was noticed that we have more than 800 units, mostly in the L.A. area but scattered widely beyond that, all with the loss-payee of D.B. Calhoun, Inc. We did some checking and we found that it's a Delaware corporation, the only stockholder of which is one Don Beverly Calhoun. I thought Peter might find this interesting.

"Holy shit," Peter said. "That's bigger than what I had read about. What he's doing is getting his followers to sign over their homes to him."

Stone replied to Arthur's e-mail.

Dear Arthur, Peter thanks you for your warm praise; he is also stunned by the size of Dr. Don's real estate holdings. In fact, I think the FBI would like very much to know about this. It smells of scam, and scam is what Dr. Don does best. May I suggest that you print out the list and send it to the director?

Come see us in England, if you have the chance. Best, Stone.

Peter left, and Stone continued going through his e-mails. He was delighted to see one of them, from the head of the Italian police department that investigated organized crime.

Dear Stone, I am pleased to let you know that, this morning, I had a call from our director of public prosecutions to tell me that Leo Casselli has agreed to a guilty plea of one count of kidnapping and accepted a prison sentence of twenty years. He will likely be out in half that time, but by then he will be passé in the business of crime. I know you will be delighted to hear this, because, since he was not tried, the five million euro reward that you and Marcel duBois posted for information leading to his trial and conviction will not have to be paid. I will give you the pleasure of notifying Mr. duBois of this turn of events. I will notify Baron Klaucke, who had hoped to claim the reward. Warm regards, Guido.

Casselli was a Mafia don who, in an attempt to extort money from the Arrington Hotels group, had kidnapped a girlfriend of Stone's. This was the best news Stone had heard for a long time, and he immediately forwarded the e-mail to Marcel and to Arthur Steele, who had agreed to reimburse them for the reward. He got immediate replies from both, and he went to lunch feeling richer, by at least two and a half million euros.

That night, in bed with Susan, he told her about the e-mails he had received.

"It sounds as though things are going well for you," she said, snuggling up, "and I am glad for that."

Stone was not quite as glad. He fell asleep with the feeling that things were going too well, and that that state of affairs could not continue.

41

The director of the FBI received a Federal Express package from Arthur Steele, whom he knew slightly, with a list of 834 real estate properties, apparently controlled by Dr. Don Beverly Calhoun. He immediately sent for Douglas Tate, his deputy director in charge of criminal investigations.

"Doug, this Calhoun creature has raised his ugly head again. I've had reports that he and two of his minions have been arraigned on illegal weapons charges in New York and Connecticut, and now I'm hearing from the head of the Steele Insurance Group that Calhoun appears to be foxing his followers out of ownership of their own homes."

"I wouldn't put him above anything," Tate replied. "I'll open a new investigation."

"You do that — and get ahold of one of the contracts he has signed with these people. I think that's where we're most likely to find illegal activity."

"Yes, sir." Tate returned to his office and checked his list of investigators who were not overburdened with work. He summoned two women, June Craven and Donna Madison, and sat them down. "What do you know about Dr. Don Beverly Calhoun?" he asked them.

Craven spoke up. "Mostly the information that appeared in a West Coast magazine a couple of years ago. The writer was later killed in a suspicious car crash on the freeway. There's a new movie called *Hell's Bells* which is supposed to be about Calhoun, but I haven't seen it yet."

"That sums up what I know, too," Madison said. "I haven't seen the movie yet, either."

"Okay, put together a team of you and four others, and start by going to the movies. Get them copies of the magazine piece, too, and read our file on Calhoun. We need to put this guy out of business."

"Yes, sir," they both said.

Walking down the hall together, Madison said, "You know, this one might actually be fun."

"Yeah," Craven replied, "and I'll bet the movie will bring some complaints out of the woodwork." Their offices were across the hall from each other, and they split up and went to work.

Dr. Don Beverly Calhoun was napping on his living room sofa after a heavy lunch, when the phone rang. "Yes?" he asked groggily.

"Dr. Calhoun," the doorman said. "A bunch of policemen are on the way up to your apartment. They didn't wait for me to buzz you."

"Thanks." Calhoun hung up and struggled to his feet. He had just time to splash some water on his face before the doorbell rang.

He opened it to find four men and two women standing in the hallway. One of the men handed him a document. "Dr. Don Beverly Calhoun, I am Lieutenant Marx of the New York State police, and this is a search warrant for these premises. Stand aside, please."

"I'd like to call my attorney," Calhoun said, unmoving.

Marx brushed past him. "You do that," he said. "All right, you two take the bedrooms, you two do the study, and we'll start in the living room. Look for a safe."

Calhoun went to the kitchen and called his attorney. "The police are here with a search warrant," he said.

"I'm not your attorney anymore, remember? Find yourself a new one, and don't expect a referral from me." He hung up.

Calhoun called his accountant. "I need a referral to a first-rate criminal lawyer," he said.

"Theodore Saxon," the accountant said, and gave him a phone number.

Calhoun called it and got Saxon on the phone. "The police are in my apartment with a search warrant," he said. "I want to hire you with immediate effect."

"Who are you?" Saxon asked.

"I am the leader of a religious group called the Chosen Few."

"Oh, yes, I saw the movie."

"It's full of lies."

"I'm sure it is. Where are you?"

Calhoun gave him the address.

"I'll be there in fifteen minutes. In the meantime, do nothing to obstruct the police, or they'll arrest you." He hung up.

Calhoun sat down at the kitchen table. He could see the police working in the living room, and they were pretty much tearing the place apart. He was glad that he had removed his two handguns to his storage unit in the building's basement.

A policeman came into the kitchen. "We're going to need the combination to your safe," he said.

"My attorney will be here shortly," Calhoun replied. "Ask me when he gets here."

The cop went back into the living room, then a female officer entered the kitchen. "You might want to go out for a cup of coffee," she said, then started opening drawers.

The doorbell rang, and Calhoun went to answer it. A short, stocky man with black hair and a matching Van Dyke beard stood there. "I am Theodore J. Saxon," he said, holding out a hand. "Call me Ted."

"Come in, Ted."

"Where are the police?"

"Everywhere," Calhoun replied, waving an arm.

Saxon marched into the living room. "Hold it!" he shouted. The police all stopped what they were doing and looked at him. "I am Dr. Calhoun's attorney. I want to see the search warrant."

"Oh, I have that," Calhoun said, taking it from his pocket and handing it to him.

Saxon scanned the document. "Proceed," he said to the cops. "It's in order." They went back to work.

Shortly, Lieutenant Marx entered the room. "I'm going to need the combination to your safe and the keys to your basement storage unit."

"Give them to him," Saxon said.

Calhoun gave him the combination and retrieved the keys to the storage unit from a kitchen drawer.

When the police walked away, Saxon took Calhoun aside. "What are they going to find in the safe?"

"Eight hundred and thirty-four deeds to houses and apartments and eight hundred thousand dollars in cash, more or less."

"How big is the fucking safe?"

"About six feet tall. It's a Fort Knox."

"What's in the storage unit?"

"Old files and two handguns."

"Are you licensed to possess handguns in New York State or New York City?"

"Ah, not exactly."

"I'll take that as a no."

"Right."

The policeman appeared at the door and crooked a finger at Calhoun, who followed him into the study, where they had opened the safe.

"What is all of that stuff?" the cop asked, pointing.

"Deeds to real estate," Calhoun replied. "The green stuff is cash."

"How much cash?"

"Eight hundred thousand dollars, give or take."

"Nothing wrong with either of those," Saxon said. "Please close the safe and forget the combination."

To Calhoun's surprise, the cops did so.

Shortly, Lieutenant Marx appeared with two Glock 9mm pistols and held them up. "Let me see your license for these."

Saxon held up a finger. "Lieutenant, the Supreme Court of the United States has ruled that citizens have the right to possess firearms in their homes, and the storage locker is an extension of Dr. Calhoun's home. That trumps New York City and State laws to the contrary. It's not as though he was carrying them on his belt."

Marx handed Calhoun the two weapons, went into the living room, and consulted with the other officers. He came back to Calhoun. "Thank you for your coopera-tion." He turned toward the living room. "Awright, we're outta here." The officers trooped out of the apartment and closed the door behind them.

Calhoun looked around the living room. "What a mess!"

"Listen, pal," Saxon said, "you've still got your deeds and cash and your handguns, too. Anything else concerning you?"

"Not at the moment," Calhoun said.

Saxon handed him a card. "I'll send you a

bill. You might want to retain me for future legal services. I'm on call twenty-four/seven."

"How much?"

"Fifty thousand dollars against fees, and I'll throw in today."

"Done," Calhoun said, and went looking for his checkbook.

42

Stone was having lunch the following day when Dino called.

"How was your flight?"

"A piece of cake. I slept most of the way. Hey, listen, I got a call from the New York State cops this morning. They went into Dr. Don's apartment with a search warrant yesterday and tore it up pretty good. They found the deeds to over eight hundred houses and apartments and eight hundred grand in cash in his safe, plus two handguns in the basement storage unit."

"Wonderful," Stone said.

"Not so wonderful. A slick lawyer named Theodore J. Saxon showed up, cited the Supreme Court ruling on guns, and they left empty-handed."

"I'm sorry to hear it. One of Arthur Steele's insurance companies insures all those residences, and Arthur sent the info to the director of the FBI yesterday. You might give the director a call and give him the location of the deeds."

"Yeah, I can do that. What's the deal with the deeds, anyway?"

"They apparently belong to Calhoun's followers. It's got to be some kind of scam."

"No doubt. I'll call the director right now."

Agents June Craven and Donna Madison were holding a meeting in a conference room at FBI headquarters.

"The director got word this morning that Dr. Don has the deeds to all those houses in a safe in his New York apartment."

An agent held up a document. "I got one of the owners to fax me his contract," he said. "What Dr. Don did is pretty smart: he refinanced all those houses and paid off the old mortgages. Since most of these people are in their fifties and sixties, they have a lot of equity, and if any of them leave the Chosen Few or displease Dr. Don, he can foreclose and they forfeit their equity."

"That can't be legal," Craven said.

"Don't be so sure. There's no evidence of duress, the property owners did it because they hold Dr. Don in high esteem."

"I've talked to a couple of dozen of these people, and I've found six who are disenchanted but are afraid to leave the cult, for fear of the wrath of Dr. Don."

"Sounds like the basis for a class-action suit," Madison said.

"Yeah, but we're not in that business."

"I'll bet we know a lawyer who'd be glad to take the case."

"You have somebody in mind?" Craven asked.

"There's this New York attorney called Stone Barrington, who's with Woodman & Weld. His son, Peter Barrington, is the director of *Hell's Bells.* How about I put a flea in his ear?"

"I can't think of anything wrong with that," Craven said.

"I've got his cell number," Madison replied.

Stone hung up his phone and called Herbie Fisher at Woodman & Weld, in New York.

"Hey, Stone, you still in England?"

"I may never come back. I've got some business for the firm, though, and I think you're just the guy to handle it." He took Herbie through the saga of Dr. Don.

"Yeah, I saw the movie — loved it."

"I'll tell Peter. I've got a list of six disaffected members of the Chosen Few who want their houses back." Stone read him the list. "Call them and see if they'd like to sign on to a class-action suit, and if all of them don't want to do it, Arthur Steele has a list of all of them, and you'll have to start cold-calling them."

"I'm on it," Herbie said.

"You and I will co-represent," Stone said. "I want my name on the suit, so Dr. Don will know I'm not through with him."

"No problem. Call me for lunch when you get back, if you ever do. I'm buying." Herbie hung up.

Stone called Dino and told him what was afoot.

"Oh, yeah, I like the sound of that," Dino said, chuckling.

"See if you can think of a few other ways to rattle Dr. Don's cage."

"I'll plumb the depths of my devious mind."

"It would be interesting to know if Dr. Don has an automobile in New York City."

"I'll bet he does."

"Maybe he has a few unpaid parking tickets?"

"Could be."

"Then you could introduce Dr. Don to the intricacies of recovering a towed vehicle from the city pound."

"I'll bet that would take up a day or two of his time."

"Let's find out."

Back at Dr. Don's apartment, he and his wife were cleaning up after the cops when he found a fistful of paper. "What the hell are these?" he demanded, showing them to Cheree.

"Oh," she said, "those are just parking tickets. They're years behind on collecting — don't worry about it."

43

Dr. Don was reviewing his e-mails in the account available to his members when he got a jolt.

Dear Dr. Don, I got a call this morning from a man who said he was an FBI agent, asking about my mortgage. He wanted to know when I took it out, how much it was for, the interest rate and the amount of the payments. He also wanted to know if I entered into the arrangement voluntarily and if I knew that, if I left the Chosen Few, I would forfeit my house to you. Is that true? If so, it's a disturbing development.

He found three more similar e-mails in his in-box. Cold sweat ensued. He sent one answer to them all:

I want you to know that everything in your mortgage is legal and proper and that you have nothing to worry about. The FBI is just harassing me through you. I've come to expect it, and I'm sorry they bothered you.

He saved the message for use in the future, if he had any more complaints. Then, later in the day he got another e-mail from the first correspondent.

Dear Dr. Don, I've had another phone call, this time from a man who said he was an attorney, asking me if I would join a class-action suit against you in the matter of my mortgage. What should I do?

He wrote back:

This is just a follow-up from the FBI call and part of their plan to harass me. Please don't concern yourself; everything is fine.

But for the remainder of the day, every time he opened his e-mail there were more such messages. He went into the bedroom where Cheree was engaged in the always-lengthy process of applying her makeup.

"Something's up," he said to her, then told her about the e-mails.

"Is that about all those deeds in the safe?"

"It is."

"Are you vulnerable?"

"Maybe — probably not."

"Then don't sweat it, just call your lawyer."

He nodded and went back to his study, fighting panic.

Stone got a call from Herbie Fisher the following day. "I've got eighteen of Dr. Don's homeowners signed up," he said. "Given my progress, if I call all of them, I'm going to have a hundred and fifty or more. Shall I continue?"

"Sure, call them all, get some help around the office."

"By now, I'm sure Dr. Don has heard from some of these people."

"Good, I don't care if he knows."

"He could be packing his bags."

"Great, I'd love for him to end up in Venezuela or Somalia — someplace really uncomfortable."

"Okay, we'll call 'em all."

Stone hung up and called Dino. "Herbie Fisher is making real progress on getting together a class for a lawsuit."

"That's great."

"I'm beginning to think that as we close in on Calhoun, he might take it on the lam,

271

as they used to say in Warner Brothers movies."

"Could be."

"Do you think you might find a way to mention to the director that Dr. Don could be a flight risk?"

"I think I could do that. If he buys it, he could probably get the guy's passport on a watch list."

"I would just love that." Stone hung up and called Herbie. "How many you got in your class so far?"

"Twenty-three."

"Go ahead and file the suit. Calhoun is at his New York apartment, as far as I know. Let him hear from us."

"What if he runs?"

"I'm working on getting his passport invalidated."

"What a good idea!"

Bright and early the following morning Dr. Don's doorbell rang, then there was hammering on the door. He got there in his pajamas. A man with a briefcase stood there.

"Dr. Don Beverly Calhoun?"

"Who are you? How did you get past the doorman?"

"I have a delivery for you," the man said, thrusting a clipboard at him. "Sign on the bottom line."

Calhoun signed. "What delivery?"

The man handed him an envelope. "You've been served, pal."

Dr. Don closed the door and turned to find Cheree standing behind him in a teddy. "What's going on? Who was that?"

Calhoun ripped open the envelope and read the first paragraph. "Class-action suit," he said. "Twenty-three complainants."

"Come back to bed — that's going to take months, if not years." She took his hand and led him back to the bedroom.

Calhoun lay on his back, staring at the ceiling, until the alarm clock went off at eight.

44

Stone asked the stables to saddle a horse for him, then he rode through the wood, across a meadow, and spurred his mount to jump the stone wall that separated his property from the Curtis estate. There were various vehicles parked in front of the big house, Susan's among them, and he thought he'd drop in and see how the work was going. A hitching post had thoughtfully been provided a century or so ago, from the look of it, and he tied his horse there.

Inside there was a mix of sounds: light machinery, a grinder of some sort, various shouts from assorted workers. He found Peter and Ben in the library, which looked to be nearly finished. "Good morning."

"Morning, Dad. We're just lining up our setups for our first day's shooting, which looks like being after the weekend." Stone left them to it and toured the other rooms. The drawing room was nearing completion, too, and large men were carrying in pieces of reupholstered furniture. He started back to the front door, and as he approached, a man appeared, peering tentatively inside. Stone recognized Leslie Bourne, Sir Charles's son. "Good morning. It's Leslie Bourne, isn't it?"

"Yes, and I recall that you are Mr. Barrington." They shook hands.

"Can I help you, Mr. Bourne?"

"Perhaps you can. I'm looking for my father."

"I think you'll find him at his cottage next door."

"Oh, not that father — I mean Sir Richard Curtis."

Stone thought that the man must not read the papers — at least, not the county papers. "I'm afraid Sir Richard is deceased."

Bourne looked as though he had been slapped. "What?" He apparently couldn't think of anything else to say. "When?"

"Some weeks ago. He was murdered in the meadow at Windward Hall."

"Murdered? By who?"

"By Brigadier Wilfred Burns."

Bourne's mouth hung open.

"The brigadier was arrested and charged, then he hanged himself in his jail cell."

"That doesn't make any sense," Bourne

said. "He and Sir Richard were the best of friends."

"It seems that everyone around here is the best of friends, until they start killing each other or themselves."

"Is that meant to be funny?"

"Merely an observation."

"I see."

"Perhaps you would like to know that your father — I'm referring to the man whose name you carry — appears to be in the last stages of his illness. Perhaps you'd like to visit him."

"I think not."

"May I ask, why did you want to see Sir Richard Curtis?"

"I'd hoped he might clear up a few things for me."

"Perhaps your father could do that."

Bourne ignored the comment. "What's going on here?" he asked.

"This house and its property have been sold to a hotel group, who plan to turn it into a country house hotel."

"What a good idea," Bourne said. "Tell me, are they looking for investors? I run what you Americans call a hedge fund."

"And what do you call it?"

"An investment group. We're always looking for places to put our clients' money. You didn't answer my question."

"I'm sorry, what was your question?"

"Are they looking for investors? The hotel group."

"No, they aren't, it's a closely held company."

"May I know its name?"

"The Arrington Group."

"Ah, yes, they're in Los Angeles and Paris and are building something in Rome, I believe."

"Your information is good."

"Perhaps you can tell me, whence the name Arrington?"

"From Arrington Calder Barrington."

"Oh? Are you a relation?"

"She was my wife, now deceased."

"I didn't know. And Calder?"

"The late actor Vance Calder, her previous husband."

"Ah, yes, Centurion Studios. We've had a go at putting some money there but were shut out."

"Yes, the studio is owned mostly by its current and retired employees. There are only a very few outsiders who own shares. Someone made a bid a few years ago, but it was rejected by a vote of the stockholders, who are very attached to the studio."

"And would you know who the outsiders are?"

"I am one of them. The others are my associates."

"Calder had a son, didn't he?"

"A stepson. I am his father."

"He must have inherited Vance Calder's shares."

"He did, or rather his trust did. Before you ask, I am his trustee."

"You seem to be involved in very interesting properties, Mr. Barrington."

"I have that good fortune."

Bourne handed him a card. "Perhaps we could have lunch sometime, when you're in London."

Stone slipped the card into his pocket. "If you'll excuse me, I have a horse waiting."

"Ah, yes, I saw him on my way in. Handsome animal."

"Yes. He was your father's before."

"Tell me, how did you come to buy Windward Hall?"

"I was introduced to Sir Charles by a mutual friend."

"I see."

"I must go. I'm sure your father would like to see you once more."

"I very much doubt it," Bourne replied.

Stone left him standing on the front steps and rode away.

45

Dr. Don came into the kitchen for breakfast and found his wife dressed to go out.

"Do you have any plans for today?" she asked.

"Nothing important. Something I can do for you?"

"I need to hit half a dozen shops, and the service doesn't have a driver available. Would you drive me around? I'm only going to need a few minutes at each place, then we can have a good lunch somewhere."

"Sure, why not?"

"Ready in half an hour?"

"Sure." Calhoun dug into his eggs.

Calhoun called down to the garage for the car and had it waiting at the curb when Cheree came down. "Where to first?"

"Let's start with Lord & Taylor, then work our way uptown."

Calhoun managed an illegal U-turn on

West Fifty-seventh Street, then turned downtown on Fifth Avenue. They were lucky with traffic and the lights and arrived at Lord & Taylor in ten minutes. Cheree went inside, and somebody pulled out of a space at the curb, so Calhoun swung in. He saw something in the store window, so he switched off the car and got out to have a look. When he turned to go back a traffic officer was standing at the rear of the car, writing a ticket. He didn't disturb her, just waited until she had taped it to the windshield and worked her way down the street. What the hell, he thought, it's already got a ticket on it, so I won't get another if I run inside for a minute.

He trotted to the men's department and asked to try on the jacket in the window. He liked it, a tailor came and marked some alterations, then he paid for it and went back outside. A UPS van was parked in the spot once occupied by his car. Jesus, had it been stolen?

The UPS driver stopped on his way into the store. "Was your car the Bentley parked there?"

"Yes. Did you see who took it?"

"Tow truck. They take them to a police garage downtown on the West Side. You can Google it for the address."

"Thank you." He sat there, steaming, until Cheree came out.

"Where's the car?"

"Towed. I have to go downtown and pay the fee to get it back."

"Oh, swell. Well, I'll hoof it up to Saks while you do that. Call me when you're ready to pick me up for lunch." She started up Fifth Avenue, while Calhoun looked for a cab; it took fifteen minutes, and he got inside gratefully. "You know the police garage downtown where your car goes when it gets towed?"

"Sure."

"Let's go there. Can I have some air-conditioning?"

"Sorry, it's broken."

The drive downtown took all of half an hour, and Calhoun had sweated through his shirt by the time they got there. He paid the driver, went inside, and presented himself at a window.

"Help you?" a man in a uniform said.

"My car was towed about forty-five minutes ago on Fifth Avenue in the Forties."

"What kind?"

"Bentley Mulsanne."

The man checked his clipboard. "Not here yet — I'd have noticed. You can wait for it."

He pointed at some uncomfortable-looking chairs.

Calhoun took a chair, one with a leatherette seat, patched with duct tape. There were half a dozen other people waiting, and it reminded him of being in the holding cell in Katonah. He took several deep breaths to calm down and cool down. No air-conditioning here, either, just a fan. An hour and two trips to the window later, he once again presented himself at the window.

"Ah, the Mulsanne," the cop said. "Not here yet."

"How long can it take for the truck to drive here from Fifth Avenue? It only took me half an hour in a cab, and it's been an hour and forty-five minutes."

"License number?"

"New York, TCF-1."

The cop turned to his computer and did a search. "Ah, here's the problem: they took it to the Queens garage."

"Queens?"

"Sometimes we get short of space here, and they get redirected." The man handed him a card with the address, and Calhoun went outside to get a cab. Nothing, and he could see for blocks. He started trudging east, and took off his jacket to cool down. Finally, he found a cab on Ninth Avenue and gave the driver the address in Queens. He called Cheree.

"Yes? You hungry?"

"Starved, but the car is at the police garage in Queens, and I'm on my way there. Go ahead and get something. I'm going to be a while."

"Okay."

He hung up and waited the forty minutes it took to get to the Queens garage through heavy traffic, then presented himself at the window. "Bentley Mulsanne, New York plate TCF-1."

"Nice ride," the cop said, and checked his clipboard. "Oh, yeah, it's upstairs. Check out with me, and I'll give you the keys."

"How much?"

"Let's see, a hundred and twenty-five for —"

"A *hundred and twenty-five dollars*?"

"That's for the ticket, plus the towing charge — that's another one-fifty." He checked his computer. "Oh, and you've got a few other tickets."

Calhoun's heart sank. "How much?"

"Let's see, there's eleven at one-twenty-five each, plus late-payment charges, comes to twenty-nine hundred bucks. Cash or credit card?"

Calhoun handed over a card. "I haven't

got that much cash on me."

The cop ran it. "Sorry, it didn't work. You got another one?"

What was going on here? He paid his bills on time. The second card worked. He signed the slip and was given the keys.

"Fourth floor, space 103," the cop said.

"Where's the elevator?"

"Out of order. The stairs are over there."

Calhoun trudged up the four airless flights and found his car. It was blocked in by two others.

"Help!" he yelled repeatedly. No one around, no keys in the cars. He went back down the stairs to the window. "My car is blocked in by two others."

"Sorry about that." The cop picked up a phone and paged somebody, then hung up. "He's on the way."

Calhoun trudged up the four flights again, and by now he was light-headed, as well as soaking wet. He got to the fourth floor just as the second car was moved, but he didn't make it to the Bentley. His knees buckled, and the lights went out.

He woke up in an ambulance, the siren going, an oxygen mask strapped to his face. The ambulance came to a stop.

Calhoun lifted the mask "Where am I?"

"Bellevue Hospital," the EMT said.

46

Calhoun was taken into the emergency room and put on an examination table in a curtained-off cubicle. A doctor who appeared to be a recent high-school graduate examined him and strapped a blood pressure cuff to his left arm. He pressed a button and the cuff inflated.

"Ow!" Calhoun yelled. "Too tight."

"Sorry about that," the kid said. "No adjustment available. Just relax and enjoy the calm."

The calm was a cacophony of screams, curses, and shouts of "Nurse!" A woman with a clipboard showed up, asked for the name and phone number of his doctor, then sat down next to his table and took an incredibly detailed history.

"I'm hot," Calhoun said. "Can you make it cooler in here?"

"Sorry about that — it gets a little cooler for a minute when someone opens the outside door."

"Can you prop the outside door open?"

"I never thought of that," she said. She left and didn't come back; it never got any cooler. The blood pressure cuff automatically reinflated every three minutes. The young doctor came back after an hour and a half and checked the recorded tape. "Your blood pressure is elevated," he said. "One forty-five over ninety."

"It usually is," Callhoun said. "What's wrong with me?"

"You may have had a heart attack," he said. "What were you doing when you fainted?"

"I had just climbed four flights of stairs twice," Calhoun replied.

"Any chest pains?"

"No, I just got dizzy."

"Well, we'll keep you on the machine for a while."

Calhoun checked his watch: after four o'clock. "Can I get out of here now?"

"We can't discharge you until your doctor arrives and signs you out."

"But I feel fine," Calhoun lied.

"We aren't going to discharge you only to have you collapse and die on our doorstep." He left the cubicle.

Calhoun tried to sleep but could only doze

fitfully. His cell phone rang; it was still on his belt. "Hello?"

"Don, it's after four. Where are you?"

"I'm in the emergency room at Bellevue."

"What's wrong?"

She wouldn't be too concerned, he thought; after all, there was eight hundred grand in the safe, and she had the combination. "I had to climb eight flights of stairs at the police garage, and I passed out. There's nothing wrong with me, but they won't discharge me until my doctor comes and signs me out. Call him, will you, and tell him to get his ass down here?"

"Okay."

"And will you go to the garage and get the car out? I've already paid twenty-nine hundred bucks for the tickets and fines."

"Will I have to climb eight flights of stairs?"

"Only four — I had to climb them twice. Make sure they send somebody up there to get the other cars out of the way." He gave her the address.

"Queens?"

"Don't ask. Tell them I'm the guy the ambulance took away. They'll remember that."

"Okay."

"Then come and pick me up here. The

doctor will have had time to get here by then."

"All right." She hung up.

The blood pressure cuff inflated again. Three hours passed, and Cheree finally showed up.

"What took you so long?"

"They had moved the car to the Manhattan garage, and I had to start all over there."

"Where's my doctor?"

"In the Bahamas," she said.

"Shit!" He pressed the call button, but no one came. "Go out there and find the doctor — the one who looks like a high-school kid — and get him in here."

Cheree left and came back half an hour later with a young Asian doctor. "Yours has gone off duty. Will this one do?"

"Yes, thank you. Doctor, unhook me from this thing. I'm leaving."

"I'm sorry, sir, but your doctor hasn't arrived to sign you out."

"He's in the Bahamas, and I'm not waiting until he gets back." He clawed at the blood pressure cuff, but it was inflating again. "Get it off me!"

"You'd better do as he says, Doctor," Cheree said, "or he'll have a heart attack."

The doctor complied. "You'll have to check yourself out and sign a form releasing the hospital from any liability."

"Gladly," Calhoun said. "Get me the fucking form."

The doctor came back half an hour later with a clipboard. "Haven't I seen you on TV?"

"Maybe." Calhoun signed the form and got up.

"Oh, yeah, you're that crazy preacher. I'm surprised you didn't have a heart attack years ago."

"Go fuck yourself," Calhoun said. He grabbed Cheree and made his way outside. "Where's the car?"

"In a garage six blocks from here. It was the closest place I could find."

47

Stone stopped into the estate office to use the copying machine, and Major Bugg spoke up. "I'm glad to see you. The housekeeper has told me we need two additional housemaids to accommodate all the guests and for their offices. We can hire part-timers until things return to normal."

"All right, go ahead," Stone said, then returned to his desk.

Bugg waited until he had left. "You ran the ad, didn't you?" he asked his assistant.

"I've got four applicants coming in this morning," she said.

"Good. Hire the first two who seem acceptable. I don't want to hear any more about it."

"Certainly."

The following morning Calhoun got out of bed feeling exhausted. The phone rang. "Hello?"

A man with a British accent said, "Dr. Don, this is Edgar Furrow, in Beaulieu."

It took Calhoun a moment. "Oh, yes." Furrow was a follower, a local builder who had done an inspection on Curtis House when he was trying to buy it. "Edgar, how are you?"

"Just fine. I read about your troubles with this Barrington fellow, and I'm sorry for it."

"Thank you."

"My daughter, Sadie, has just gotten a job at Windward Hall as a housemaid. She'll be working there for the next three months, at least."

"That's very interesting, Edgar."

"I'd hoped you would think so. If you like, I can get her to give you written reports on what goes on there."

"I'd like that very much, Edgar. Have Sadie e-mail them directly to me." He gave the man his e-mail address, then hung up.

He went in to breakfast, and Cheree set down his bacon and eggs. "It's time for us to go to Rio," he said to her.

She sat down and stared at him. "Are you serious?"

"Can't you see? Everything is going to hell. I've been arrested three times, we've been thrown out of England, this apartment has been searched, and it's all because of

292

Barrington. I suspect that thing yesterday with the car had something to do with him, too, though I don't know what."

"But *Rio?*"

"We may not have to stay long, but that's why I bought the apartment there, in case we had to get out in a hurry. It's completely furnished, and the freezer is full of food."

"When had you thought of going?"

"Immediately. Well, almost immediately. Don't worry about packing a lot, you can shop for new clothes there."

"All right," she said, "as long as it's temporary. After all, they're not after me."

"You're next," he said. He finished breakfast, went into his study, and found a phone number on his computer. He hesitated before making the call, because the man scared him: he was so bland and nondescript-looking but he was lethal, and Calhoun always had the feeling that he could turn on him at any moment.

"This is Al Junior," he said.

"This is Dr. Don. I need you for a special job."

"Tell me about it."

"You'll need to leave the country. It could take a few days or a few weeks."

"How many weeks?"

"Two should be enough. I need you in

New York tonight, and bring your passport. How early can you get here?"

"I can get a flight this morning," he said. "I should be there by eight o'clock."

"Then I'll meet you at Kennedy. Book yourself on a night flight to London. They usually have one around ten o'clock, and your luggage will go straight through. Don't bring any tools with you — those will be provided at the other end."

"I see. I'm going to need fifty thousand in cash up front and another fifty when I'm done. More, if it takes longer than two weeks."

"I'll meet your flight from L.A. and give you the first payment. Be sure you declare the cash with customs. I know from experience: forgetting that can be expensive. E-mail me your flight times, and take your cell phone with you, it will work there."

"Will do."

They both hung up.

Calhoun dreaded meeting the man.

They met at the gate, went to a nearby bar, and found a corner table out of earshot of other travelers.

"Details, please," Al Jr. said.

Calhoun took a deep breath. He had used Al Jr. only once before, for the job on the magazine writer's car. He ran a pawnshop that had a big gun business in L.A.; word was he had inherited both the business and his sideline from his father, Al Sr. "The last name Barrington: Stone, the father, Peter the son."

"Got it."

"When you arrive in London rent a car and drive to a village called Beaulieu." Calhoun pronounced it for him, then gave him a page ripped from a driving atlas of Britain. "There are two houses south of the village, here and here. The properties are next door to each other. The Barringtons live in the one to the north, Windward Hall. The son is making a film at the one to the south, Curtis House. It's been mentioned in the entertainment pages.

"From the airport, call a man named Edgar Furrow, who lives in Beaulieu. He will make a hotel reservation for you. His daughter, Sadie, works at Windward Hall, and she can give you the layout. Edgar also has sources for weapons. You can call me on my cell phone if absolutely necessary, or you can e-mail me." He gave the man a card with the number and the address.

"Anything special to tell me?"

Calhoun thought about that. "Yes. Do the son first. I want the father to know he's dead."

"As you wish."

"Good luck," Calhoun said, then walked away, feeling better, relieved.

48

Al Jr. settled down in first class, had a couple of bourbons, avoided the fish and chose the steak, washed down with two glasses of wine. He enjoyed travel at the expense of others, and he was looking forward to England.

At Heathrow an immigration officer asked him, "Business or pleasure?"

"A little of both." He cleared customs, changed some money, then found a phone and called Furrow.

"I've booked you a room at the best hotel in town," Furrow said, giving him the name and address.

"Make it a suite," Al said. He then went to a rental car desk and asked for a Mercedes, got an E-class sedan with a GPS; he entered the hotel's address, and half an hour later he had cleared the airport and was turning onto the motorway south. He longed for a shower, a shave, and a long nap.

At the hotel he checked in, and as he turned from the desk a large, ruddy-faced man approached him. "Al? I'm Edgar Furrow. Can I buy you some breakfast?"

"Just coffee. I had breakfast."

They sat down in the restaurant. "I was told you might need tools. Anything special?"

"Can you obtain exotics?"

"How exotic?"

"Ideally, a smallish nine-millimeter handgun and a sniper rifle, with a fitting for a tripod and an eight-power scope, and that will break down and fit into a briefcase — both of them silenced."

"The silencers are no problem. I'll have to inquire about the other."

Al gave him his cell number. "Call me after noon. I need to sleep until then."

"Don't you want to know the lay of the land?"

Al sat back. "Sure."

Furrow unfolded a hand-drawn map and showed him where the two houses were located. "My daughter, Sadie, works at Windward Hall. She says there are a lot of movie people in and out of there all the time. The son and his partner work in an office in the southwest corner of the ground floor, and the father has an office next door to them."

"How do they move between the two houses?"

"Most of them drive, both the father and the son have taken to riding horses. They take a trail through the wood here, they jump a stone wall here, then ride to Curtis House. Sometimes they go together, sometimes alone."

"What time of day?"

"They leave Windward Hall around eight in the morning and return around six. The father doesn't stay all day, sometimes he'll take a ride around the Curtis property."

"Is either of them armed?"

Furrow laughed. "You're in Britain, where guns are rare, except for shotguns. I have a military source — the army is all over Salisbury Plain, north of here."

"Anywhere around I can rent a horse?"

"The nearest place is ten miles or so."

"How about a bicycle?"

"There's a very good shop in the town, in the high street, where you can hire or buy. It's next door to a bank."

"I came down here from Heathrow on the motorway, past Southampton. Is that the best way back?"

"It's the fastest."

"Is there a back route?" He took the map Calhoun had given him from a pocket.

"You can go north across Salisbury Plain and connect with the M4 motorway west of Heathrow, here, or you can navigate cross-country."

Al thanked the man and gave him his cell number. "Call me if there's anything I should know."

"Certainly."

Al collected his luggage and found his suite; it was small but comfortable. He undressed and got into bed and was still sleeping when the phone rang. "Yes?"

"It's me. Your tools will be ready tomorrow this time of day. Someone is modifying them to your specifications. There'll be a box of ammo for each of them. Do you need a holster for the nine?"

"Something to wear on my belt would be good."

"Done."

"I don't want to meet at the hotel again."

"On the road toward Windward Hall there's a pub called the Rose & Crown. Meet me there at two o'clock tomorrow in the saloon bar. It'll be quiet at that hour."

"I'll find it." Al hung up, showered, shaved, and dressed, then left the hotel, with directions to the high street. He found the bicycle shop, and it was a good one, also selling maps, travel books, and birding equipment. He asked the clerk to show him a good touring bike and selected a Raleigh five-speed. He chose a roomy set of saddle-bags, as well, and picked out a large, comfortable seat. "Will you take American dollars?" he asked the clerk.

"You'll get a better exchange rate at the bank next door," the man said. "Your bike will be ready to go in twenty minutes. Oh, and you'll need a lock, unless you plan to keep it indoors."

"You have binoculars?" Al asked. "I'd like to do some birding." He looked at some, chose a ten-power pair, and bought a tripod, as well, then he went next door, changed three thousand dollars for pounds, went back, and rode away on his new bike, whistling a tune, the binoculars and tripod in a saddlebag. He rode out of town, past the Rose & Crown, then found the gates to Windward Hall and Curtis House.

He didn't go inside; he would do that later.

49

Calhoun was going through his files, deciding what to take with him and what to shred, when his cell phone rang. "Hello?"

"I'm on-site," Al Jr. said. "Your man here seems to have everything in hand. I've been out there and looked over the estates from the road. The setup is good for an outdoor event. I'll try for that — it's a lot less time consuming than getting inside."

"Sounds good," Calhoun said. "Keep me posted. I may be leaving the country soon, but my cell phone will work wherever I am."

"Right." Al hung up.

Calhoun found himself breathing faster. He took a catalog case from his luggage rack and packed the cash into it, then put it into the safe. He packed the deeds into four large FedEx boxes and addressed them to his secretary at his L.A. office.

He packed some clothes into two cases; those, his briefcase, and the catalog case would make up all that he would take with him. Anything else he needed he either already had in the Rio apartment or could buy there.

Cheree came to the door and saw his luggage. "You're serious about this, then?"

"Did you ever doubt it?"

"Well, I guess I'd better get packed, too."

"Try not to take too much." She always took too much. "Think of how you'll enjoy the shopping."

"Are we taking the cash?"

"We are, and there's more stashed in Rio."

Al left his hotel and bicycled to the Rose & Crown, arriving early for his meeting with Furrow. He consulted the menu and ordered a lunch of steak and kidney pie and a pint of bitter. Both were good.

Furrow arrived on time, carrying a black aluminum briefcase, which he set under the table until a few people had left the room. When they were alone he set the briefcase on the table and opened it. Al was impressed. "Somebody made this?" he asked, removing the stockless, barrel-less, pistol-gripped guts of the rifle.

"No, I'm told it's a special sniper's rifle, made to the army's specifications. It fires a

.223 round, high-velocity. The scope is ten-power."

"That's okay, I've got a tripod already."

"The pistol is a general officer's model, compact." It fit into the case, too. "The silencers, my man made. All this has to go back to the armory when you're done with it. He can't have it missing if somebody takes inventory, and no policeman will ever think to look for it in a military armory."

"Fair enough," Al said. "I wouldn't want to carry it through security or customs, anyway."

"I should think not. Would you like some lunch?"

"Thanks, I've already had mine. I need to do some sighting in."

"Be careful with that — don't be seen."

"Of course not, and I'll use the silencers, too."

"Very good."

Al got up, shook Furrow's hand, and took the briefcase with him. The case fit nicely into his saddlebag, and the cover closed over it. He pedaled down the road, past the Windward Hall gate and almost to the Curtis House entrance, where he stopped, looked and listened for traffic, then lifted the bicycle over the stone wall and vaulted over. He took the case from the saddlebag,

304

slung his binoculars around his neck, and stuffed his birding book into a jacket pocket.

The wood was only a few yards away; he left the bicycle leaning against the inside of the stone wall and set off through the trees. After a few minutes he came to the riding trail and crossed it, then passed a small wooden house. He peeked through a window and found it deserted, then continued on until he saw clear daylight ahead, beyond the trees.

He picked a spot from which he could fire between trees to a spot on the stone wall that separated the two properties. He could see that the riding trail left the woods and wound down to the wall, the grass pounded flat by recent hoofs. He set down the briefcase and walked to the edge of the wood and brought his binoculars to bear, first on Windward Hall, in the distance, then, slightly nearer, on Curtis House, where there was much activity.

Trucks and cars were parked in the forecourt, and men came and went, carrying tools and materials. He could hear the sounds of power tools coming from the house, a good thing, cover for him.

He went back to where he had left the case, opened it, and removed and assembled the rifle. The barrel was slightly shorter than he would have liked, but it made the weapon more easily concealable. He loaded a magazine, shoved it into the rifle, and sighted toward the stone wall, picking a spot where the hoof marks ended. Excellent; he would be shooting from behind the horsemen.

He sighted through the weapon then looked around at trees, gauging the wind direction and speed. There wasn't much of either. He picked a stone on the top of the wall, sighted it in, and squeezed off a round. The silencer was very effective, and he watched through the scope as his round ricocheted off the stone below the one where he had aimed. He made a small adjustment to the sight and repeated the process, striking the stone dead center.

Then he heard the sound of hooves on turf.

50

Billy Barnett, née Teddy Fay, woke at seven o'clock, as if by an alarm. His wife slept soundly on. Since breakfast was prepared and brought to their room she didn't have to get up and make it, as she did at home.

Billy shaved carefully and gave some thought to allowing a mustache to sprout. He left his upper lip unshaven. He dressed in the riding clothes he had bought in the village and was sitting at their little table when the maid brought what the locals called "a full English breakfast." He woke his wife with a kiss, and she joined him for their morning meal.

"So what will your day be like?" she asked him, her mouth full of toast.

"I'll take a ride over to the Curtis place with Stone and Peter and have a look at how the work is going there."

"That interests you?"

"Building is one of my many interests."

"Do they need any guarding here? Is that why you're going?"

Billy shook his head. "They're safe enough, since the Reverend Don got run out of the country, and all his people with him."

"I'm glad to hear it."

They finished breakfast and Billy walked downstairs and out the rear door of the house to the stables, where the three horses had been saddled for their riders. They snorted, and their breath could be seen in the chill morning air. Billy greeted his mount with a stroke of the neck and offered her a sugar cube, which the horse quickly made disappear.

Peter appeared first, stretching his body and yawning, and Stone arrived soon after. They mounted and trotted off across the broad meadow before Windward Hall. They took the trail through the wood and emerged a hundred yards from the stone wall. Stone and Peter took the wall abreast, while Billy followed a few yards back. He was about to spur his horse on for the jump when something he saw ahead made him rein up and dismount.

He approached the stone wall and reached out to feel the two marks, one on a lower stone, one at the top of the wall. They were the marks of bullets striking the stone, and they hadn't been there yesterday. Billy turned and looked back the way they had come, then focused his attention on the wood.

Al watched the third man, who had spoiled his aim, as he dismounted and inspected the wall. It had never occurred to him that someone might notice the marks where his bullets had struck. He watched as the man looked back, then trained his attention on the wood. Al shrank back behind a tree and saw the man walking toward him, leading his horse. He moved to another tree, then another. The man came relentlessly on, his eyes raking the edge of the wood. Al turned and ran back as far as the empty little house and waited there. If the man approached this far, he would kill him.

Billy walked through the first trees, his eyes sweeping the area, particularly the ground. He had gone only a few yards when the gleam of something in the sunlight got his attention. He bent and picked it up, then sniffed it. He avoided looking farther into the wood, because he knew a man was waiting there with a rifle. Rather, he slipped the brass shell casing into his jacket pocket, remounted his horse, and ran her toward the wall, clearing it easily, then rode on toward the house and its collection of parked workmen's vehicles. He dismounted, tied his horse to a hitching post, and went into the house in search of Stone. He found him talking earnestly with Susan Blackburn, who held a book of wallpaper.

Billy waited until they had finished their conversation, then caught Stone's eye and with a motion of his head, beckoned him into the hallway.

"What's up, Billy?" Stone asked.

Billy fished the casing from his pocket and handed it to Stone. "I found two bullet marks in the stone wall, and I walked into the wood far enough to come across this."

"Two-two-three?"

"Right — a military round."

"I thought the army were all up on Salisbury Plain, not down here. Any idea when this was left in the wood?"

"The marks weren't on the wall yesterday," Billy replied. "I'd guess this morning. I think someone was further back in the wood, but I wouldn't pursue an armed man into the trees. Are there any firearms in the house?"

"Half a dozen shotguns and a couple of deer rifles. They're in a concealed case in

310

the study."

"With your permission, I'd like to arm myself and have a look around the wood."

"Of course. Be careful, and for God's sake don't shoot anybody if you can possibly avoid it, and if you can't, don't kill him. The police around here don't spend a lot of time dealing with men dead of gunshot wounds. They'd be all over us for days." Stone explained how to open the gun closet.

"Well, I don't want to make their day," Billy replied, "but I will search the wood."

"Do it carefully," Stone said. "Do you want company?"

"No, thank you." Billy left the house and got back onto his horse.

Al watched Billy through the trees as he rode back toward Windward Hall, and he breathed a sigh of relief. He thought he might wait for the two Barringtons to return; maybe he'd get a shot, after all.

51

Billy found the button under the mantel-piece and pressed it; the panel to his right swung open, revealing a rack of weapons. Billy chose one of the two deer rifles, found a box of cartridges, and loaded the gun with thirty-ought-six rounds. He went outside, remounted his horse, and, resting the rifle across his lap, rode off toward the wood.

He rode as far as the hermitage, got down and tied the reins to a tree branch, then he stood still and listened. From his right, toward the road, he heard what could have been a footstep. He listened again but heard nothing, so he started through the wood toward the road, moving carefully and quietly. Silence made for slow going, but soon he heard a noise — something metallic scraping on something hard. He quickened his pace, not worrying about the noise. Shortly, the stone wall along the road came into sight, but he saw nothing else. He ran to the wall, leaned over it, and looked up and down the road, first to his left, then the right. He caught a glimpse of motion to his right and concentrated, but it was gone. Billy closed his eyes and tried to replay what he had seen. It wasn't much: a man on a bicycle, disappearing around a bend in the road. He concentrated: big man, broad shoulders, thick neck, wool cap. That was it. Billy stayed on the estate side of the wall; no point in chasing a man on a bicycle.

He looked around the ground on his side of the wall, then at the wall itself. He found a smidge of green paint on a stone, smaller than his little fingernail. A green bicycle. That cut the search to half the two-wheelers in the country, he reckoned. Billy walked back to his horse, went to the house, unloaded and put away the rifle.

Stone and Peter returned to the house for lunch, and Peter excused himself to wash up; Billy was already at the table when Stone came in and sat down. "See anything?"

"A man was watching us from the wood this morning, and we know he had a rifle. I rode out as far as the hermitage and tracked him back to the road: just missed him. I caught a glimpse of a large man on a bicycle

313

as he rode out of sight around a bend. That's it."

"You think we have something to worry about?"

"I do."

"What do you suggest?"

"I think he'll be back, probably tomorrow morning. I'll see if I can get there first. Don't ride over there tomorrow — drive."

"All right."

Peter joined them, and they changed the subject.

Al got back to his hotel suite breathless and sweaty, so much so that he took a drink, something he rarely did before the cocktail hour. He sat down in an easy chair and reviewed his experience, and he was satisfied that no one had seen or heard his test shots fired; it just wasn't possible. It was the third man who screwed up things. He had gotten in the way of Al's firing line and inspected the wall, then looked toward the wood, where Al awaited in the trees. Al had ducked behind a tree, and the man came on, on foot, but he showed no sign of seeing anything.

Al reached into a pocket for the brass he had policed and found only one shell casing. He stood up and dug into all his pockets, looking for the second one, but he found nothing. He had a clear memory of picking up both shells, but he had been interrupted by the approaching man. Had he dropped one? And even if he had done so, had the man found it? The floor of the wood was carpeted in all sorts of ground cover — ivy, pine seedlings, other things. It would be easy for a shell casing to get lost in there.

He went over his flight to the bicycle, getting it over the wall and vaulting over. He had struck the wall with the bicycle, making a sound. Had it left a mark? He had looked back from down the road and seen a movement, not much, but enough to be a man emerging from the wood. His only remedy at this point would be to go back and find the shell casing. After all, he knew approximately where it was.

The bourbon began to relax him, and his fears subsided somewhat. That was what he'd do. He'd go back tomorrow and find the casing, then he'd know his presence in the wood had gone undetected. He thought about calling Dr. Don and confiding in him, but he dismissed the idea out of hand. Such a call would show fear and indecisiveness on his part — not the sort of thing he would want communicated to someone who had hired him and was paying him a stiff fee.

No, he'd go out early tomorrow, before dawn, and police the wood for the shell casing. He'd rethink his whole plan and make it right, perhaps even better. Next time, he'd shoot all three of them, if he had to.

52

Dr. Don Beverly Calhoun sat at the breakfast table, reading the morning papers. He finished the *Times,* then *Daily News,* and to his regret, found picked up the what he had been looking for. **MAD EVANGELIST VISITED BY THE POLICE. AGAIN.** Mad? This upset him. Did people really think that of him? Whatever; it was time to act. He went into his study, looked up a number, and called the charter company with whom he held a quarter of a share of a Citation CJ4. "This is Dr. Calhoun," he said.

"Good morning, Dr. Don," the woman replied. "What can we do for you today?"

"I'm going to need a larger aircraft," he said.

"Are you reaching for a new destination? Something beyond the CJ4?"

"Rio."

"Well, let's see, that's a little over four

thousand nautical miles. That would require two fuel stops in the CJ4, being conservative."

"What would it take to go nonstop?" He had visions of getting successfully out of the country, then being arrested at a fuel stop. "What about a Gulfstream 450?"

"Lovely airplane, with a range of 4,350 nautical miles. Even in that you'd be cutting it close to go nonstop. You'd really need a Gulfstream 550 for that distance. May I make a suggestion?"

"Go right ahead."

"We've recently received a new Citation Latitude, one of the first off the line. She has a very comfortable wide-body cabin with six feet of headroom, and a range of 2,700 nautical miles. She could do just one fuel stop, say one of the Caribbean islands, then on to Rio, and she wouldn't cost you anything like the 550, or, come to that, even the 450. The Latitude might be the ideal compromise."

"I've read about that airplane in the aviation magazines. Sounds good."

"When did you contemplate traveling, and will your wife accompany you?"

"Oh, it's not for us, we're sending a couple of employees down to do some business. I'd like for them to go tomorrow morning."

"Let me check." A pause, and the sound of a keyboard being tapped. "Yes, we can do that: say, an eight AM departure? It's going to be a good eight-hour flight, plus the fuel stop, in, shall we say, Aruba? The good news is, you remain in the same time zone, so there'll be no jet lag, the way there would be on a transatlantic crossing."

"That's fine."

"May I have your employees' names?"

"Herman Carter and Cheylyn Stefan."

"You'll have to spell that last one for me, and I'll need their dates of birth and passport numbers. We have to file them a day ahead of the flight with the IACRA program."

"Hold on a minute, and I'll get them." He went to his safe and extracted the two passports from a file, then returned and read her the information.

"And the expiration dates of their passports?"

He gave her those and their addresses.

"Good, that's all we need. We'll have provisions for two meals each aboard, and let me give you a price, with credit for your CJ4, of course." She tapped some more keys and gave him the number.

"That's fine. You can use the credit card you have on file."

"Perfect, Dr. Don. We'll look forward to seeing them aboard. They'll have two pilots and a flight attendant."

"Thank you." Calhoun hung up and went back to the kitchen, where Cheree was putting their breakfast dishes into the dishwasher. "We're on for eight AM tomorrow," he said.

"How long is the flight?"

"Two legs, about four hours each, plus one fuel stop."

"Why can't we go nonstop?"

"Because we'd need a Gulfstream 550. We've got a very nice new airplane called a Latitude, and it's half the money. That's good motivation for a fuel stop."

"I guess so."

"You don't sound very happy about this."

"What, about fleeing the country ahead of the cops?"

"We're not fleeing the country ahead of the cops. We're not about to be arrested."

"That's not what the News said this morning."

"Fuck the News," he said angrily. "What do they know?"

"The charter company has to report our names to the Feds. What if they stop us?"

"We're using different passports, a couple of people who work for me, who look enough like us for their photographs to work. They were chosen for the resemblance."

"And what is the apartment like?"

"You're going to love it. I bought the place right after the Olympics at a great price. Seven rooms and a view of Rio that won't quit."

"Does it have furniture?"

"Completely furnished by the best decorator in Brazil, and there's a Mercedes in the garage."

Cheree sighed. "Well, I guess it'll have to do."

53

Stone and Susan lay in bed, panting and sweating. It was shortly after dawn, and that is very early at the latitude at which Britain exists. She had waked him and quite easily seduced him.

"That was marvelous," Susan said.

"Bit of British overstatement?"

She laughed. "Take your compliments where you find them, sir."

"Thank you very much. Just for comparison's sake, I thought it was *bloody* marvelous — from my point of view."

"And thank *you* very much."

"You're very welcome."

She sighed. "I wish this could go on and on, but it can't. And it's all your fault."

Stone turned toward her. "There were two statements in that sentence, and I didn't understand either of them."

"It can't go on, because I've gotten so fucking busy," she said. "I've gotten to the point where I can hand over Curtis House to one of my new deputies, albeit with qualms, and now I have to go and make some sense of what's happening in London, and that's the part that's all your fault."

"Busy, I understand. I can work with that, but what's all my fault?"

"Busy is all your fault. You've given me so much good business advice that my workload has increased markedly. Before, when I was just a successful interior designer, I could do pretty much as I pleased with my day. Now, suddenly, I'm a design tycoon, and I have to drive back to London at the crack of dawn and learn to delegate authority, something I'm entirely unaccustomed to and very uncomfortable with."

"Delegating authority was supposed to give you more free time."

"And maybe it will, once I learn to do it. Just look at the Curtis House project. I have this wonderful opportunity — one that you engineered — to have my work on movie screens all over the world, and just when I'm at the point where I can start to enjoy it, I have to hand it over to somebody I hardly know and go back to London so I can begin doing it all over again. What I keep asking myself is, how does Ralph Lauren do it?"

"By delegating authority, I should think."

"There's that expression again! I'm learning to hate it!"

"Embrace it. It will give you time to embrace me."

"Oh, I'll have to delegate someone to do that, while I embrace a new client or a new project."

"Oh. Whom did you have in mind for the task?"

She pummeled his shoulder with her fists. "Dammit, I don't want to delegate you, just as I don't want to delegate anything else. I'd rather do everything myself, including you."

"You'll wear yourself out doing that."

"Yes, but it would be such fun. The only fun I have now is watching my bank balance — and my debt — climb."

"Don't worry, your bank balance will outrun your debt."

"I know it will, and so does my bank manager. He used to be just a nice man who occasionally gave me an overdraft. Now he's turned into a fawning, drooling sycophant who can't do enough for me and wants to take me to lunch!"

"Well, that's the kind of bank manager to have, isn't it?"

"I suppose I'll just have to get used to it,"

she said.

"That's the way to handle it."

"I went through my appointment book last night, and I don't have a single hour free for the next twelve days. It's all taken up with appointments with new clients and new projects and new assistants, and I have the feeling that when the twelve days are up I'll be faced with twelve weeks without an hour for myself or you. My analyst is worried for me."

"You have an analyst?"

"I do now!"

"You don't seem like the type to need an analyst."

"I didn't used to need an analyst, but now I need a shoulder to cry on. That's all she's for, really — she never gives me any useful advice. She just says thing like, 'Go somewhere for a holiday,' and I don't have time for a holiday."

"Then blow the whole thing," Stone said. "Sell your business and come live with me."

"But I love my business," she wailed. "I love you, too, of course, but now I have to choose between you and my wonderful new business, and I'm choosing the business!"

"You are?"

"That's what I've been trying to tell you for the last ten minutes. You, sir, are toast, and I can't do a thing about it. I'm a complete captive of my own success, and that, of course, is all your fault!"

"Oh, we're back to that?"

"We are. You are the victim of your own success in advising me. You are the architect of your own dumping."

Stone rolled over and stared at the ceiling. "This is such a nice ceiling," he said. "I love what you've done with it."

"*Everybody* loves what I've done with *everything*! That is my cross to bear." She got out of bed and began throwing things into a suitcase. "And now I have to go back to London and bear it." She came over to the bed, sat down, and gave him a big, wet kiss. "Goodbye, you lovely man, and thank you for this fresh, new hell." Then she grabbed her suitcase and walked out of the room.

Stone continued staring at the ceiling. "What have I done?" he asked himself.

54

Billy sat on the steps of the hermitage, huddled inside his coat against the chill of the English dawn. It was time to greet his stalker.

He picked up the deer rifle, worked the bolt to pump a round into the chamber, set the safety, tucked it under an arm, and began walking, watching his footsteps carefully to avoid the crunch of a twig or some other noise that might announce his presence sooner than he wished it to be known. He had timed it better than he had thought.

As he reached the edge of the wood, just short of the stone wall along the road, he heard from a distance the crunch of tire on gravel as the bicycle rounded the bend in the road. It was, perhaps, fifty yards away. He melted back into the trees and concealed himself, maintaining a view of the wall, remembering the spot of green paint on the stones. Billy pulled up his muffler to cover his mouth and nose, as his breath turned to mist as it was exhaled. The bicyclist was making mist as he approached.

Billy's first impression had been right. He was big, over six feet, thickset, especially at the shoulders and neck. He might have been a linebacker in his youth. The man lifted his bicycle over the wall, then put both his hands on top of the stone and vaulted over it, landing well.

Billy stepped out of the trees, the rifle at the ready. "Good morning," he said.

The man froze in his tracks, his arms at his sides. Whatever weapon he carried was not instantly available to him, as he was wearing a buttoned-up tweed coat. "What?" he said.

"I'm going to offer you two choices," Billy said.

The man said nothing, simply stared at him.

Billy knew his mind was racing, looking for survival.

"Relax," he said. "There is no way out. Get used to that."

"Out of what?"

"Out of here alive, except by the means I propose."

"What are you proposing?"

"First, I'm going to ask you some questions, which you must answer truthfully. I already know the answers to some of them, enough so that if you lie, I'll know. Lying will be fatal. Do you understand?"

"Yes," he replied without hesitation.

"Is the rifle in a case in your saddlebags?"

"Yes."

"With one hand, remove the case and throw it a few feet in my direction. Do it carefully."

The man complied. The aluminum case landed with a soft thud near Billy's feet.

"Good. Now lean against the wall and try to relax. Keep your hands away from your pockets."

He leaned against the wall and folded his hands in front of him.

"Now the questions: What is your name?"

"Al."

"Surname?"

"Greenberg."

"Where do you live, Al?"

"Los Angeles."

"Do you have a front?"

"I have a pawnshop and gun business. This work is a sideline."

"Who hired you? I warn you, this is one of the questions I know the answer to."

"A man named Calhoun."

"Correct answer. Now, here's your first

choice: you may return to your hotel, pack your bags, then get out of Beaulieu and the country. Lots of flights to the States around midday — be on one of them. Do you understand?"

"Yes."

"Here's the alternative."

"I know the alternative."

"Let me spell it out for you, so there's no room for misunderstanding: the alternative is for you to die before you hit the ground."

"I understand that."

"How much is Calhoun paying you?"

"Fifty grand."

"How much up front?"

"All of it."

"Good. That makes your next choice easier."

"My next choice?"

"That happens when you return to L.A."

"I don't understand."

"Calhoun is going to want his money's worth or want it back."

"Yeah, sure."

"Eventually, he'll send somebody to get it."

"I suppose."

"You can keep the money, if you're still willing to kill someone."

Al frowned. "Who?"

"Why, Calhoun, of course."

Al smiled a little. "Of course."

"Now I'll make you a promise: if Calhoun isn't dead, say, a month from today, I'll find you and kill you. Do you believe me?"

Al gulped. "Yes."

"All right, now you can get back on your bicycle and start your journey. But first, leave the handgun."

Al unbuttoned his coat and pulled it back to reveal the pistol in a shoulder holster. He extracted it with his thumb and forefinger and tossed it next to the rifle case.

"Goodbye," Billy said. "Until we meet again — or not."

Al nodded, picked up the bicycle, and set it down on the other side of the stone wall. Then he vaulted the wall, turned the bicycle around, hopped on it, and pedaled away. Just before he turned the first bend, he lifted a hand and gave a little wave. He didn't look back.

Billy marked a month from today in his mental calendar, then picked up the weapons and walked back to Windward Hall, looking forward to a full English breakfast.

55

Stone came down for breakfast, feeling thick-headed and slightly off. He helped himself to bacon and eggs from the buffet and sat down. A moment later he was joined by Billy Barnett.

"Good morning," Billy said. "Peter and Ben were up early, and they've already ridden over to Curtis House."

Stone stared at him. "You let them . . ."

"Relax," Billy said. "The threat has been removed."

"How so?"

"Nonviolently. He's headed for Heathrow as we speak."

"You let him go free?"

"You asked me not to kill him. What was the alternative?"

"Well, I suppose . . ."

"Don't worry, he won't trouble you again. He's even going to do a little favor for you."

"What favor?"

"I'll tell you when it happens."

"Do you have any idea who he is?"

"I know exactly who he is," Billy said. "Alvin Greenberg Junior. His father was Al Senior, who is reputed, in certain circles, to be the assassin who removed Ben 'Bugsy' Siegel from the scene, some decades ago. He ran a gun shop, now run by Al Junior. Both father and son are said to be very good at their work."

"If he's so good, how did you stop him?"

Billy shrugged. "I got there first. The rest was easy. I just offered him an opportunity to continue his life by leaving the country and not bothering us again."

"What would you have done if he hadn't agreed?"

"Then, having made the threat, I would have had to kill him."

"I'm glad it didn't come to that."

"So am I. It would have been messy."

Stone changed the subject, then left the table.

Billy got up and went downstairs to find Major Bugg, who was working at his desk. "Good morning, Major." Billy sat down across from him.

"What can I do for you this morning?"

"Just some information, please. Have you recently employed anyone new to work in the household?"

"Yes, I employed a young woman from the village to help with the housekeeping."

"Just the one?"

"Yes."

"Did you know her beforehand?"

"I knew her father — still do."

"Is he a military man?"

"Was. He's retired and owns a construction business. He did some of the work on the remodeling of this house."

"Would he be the sort who would maintain his military connections?"

"Oh, yes, he goes to all the reunions, has a lot of friends on Salisbury Plain."

"May I have his name and address?"

Bugg gave it to him. "May I ask what this is about?"

"I believe his daughter may have provided information about what goes on here to someone who meant us harm."

"I am shocked to hear that," Bugg said, and he truly looked it. "What should I do about it?"

"Just don't employ him again, and discharge the daughter. She'll know why. Leave the rest to me."

"I'll speak to her immediately."

"No, give it an hour or so."

"As you wish."

Billy thanked him and left his office. He got into his rental car and tapped the address into the GPS, then drove into town. He found the man's building yard, then took a shopping bag from the boot and went to his office, where he found the ex-officer working at his desk.

The man looked up. "Can I help you?"

Billy sat down across from him. "I've come to tell you that your attempt to help an assassin has failed."

The man didn't blink. "And you are . . . ?"

"It doesn't matter." Billy took the gun case and the pistol from the shopping bag and placed them on the man's desk.

"What's this?"

"You know very well what it is. I thought you'd like the opportunity to return these things to the armory from which you borrowed them."

"I don't know what you mean."

"Of course you do," Billy said, rising. "I'm going to let matters rest as they are, but you will no longer receive contracts from Windward Hall or Curtis House, and your daughter is being discharged as we speak."

The man looked surprised for the first time.

"We won't have a problem in the future, will we?"

"Ah . . ."

"Say it."

"No, you won't have a problem with me or my daughter in the future."

"Good. That way you will both avoid unpleasant consequences." Billy walked out of the building, closing the door behind him, then drove back to Windward Hall.

56

Al made a noon flight from Heathrow to Los Angeles and managed a first-class seat. He accepted two mimosas from the flight attendant before takeoff and as soon as they were at cruise altitude, had the first of a series of Gentleman Jacks. The bourbon went to all the right places, and he did his best to keep it there.

After the meal and a couple of glasses of wine he managed to fall into a deep sleep, not regaining full consciousness until the landing gear lowered with a jerk. He collected his luggage in a fog of hangover, made it through customs and immigration without fuss, and got a cab home. By the time he had let himself into the apartment above the store and tossed down some hair of the dog, his attention was fully focused on the problem of Dr. Don Beverly Calhoun. He regarded the man as the source of his trouble and humiliation in England.

Dr. Don made it to Teterboro the following morning on time for his flight — not that it mattered, because the flight would go when he said it should. One of the crew — a pilot whom he recognized from an earlier flight on his CJ4, examined his passport and gave him a curious look, but he asked no questions. Same with Cheree. They and their baggage were quickly settled in. Dr. Don had taken the precaution of filling out a customs form online, declaring the eight hundred thousand dollars he carried in cash, but under his employee's name, which matched the passport. It was not illegal to carry large sums of cash abroad, as long as it was declared, and he figured that there was a large stack of those forms waiting to be scrutinized at some customs office. He would be in Rio by the time they got around to his.

They settled into the comfortable cabin of the new airplane, which offered the size and space of a larger aircraft, and waited for the pilots to work through their checklists and get a clearance for their flight. As they waited, Calhoun's cell phone buzzed on his belt. He was mystified for a moment as to who might have that number, but then he remembered Al. Good news, no doubt.

"Hello?"

"It's Al."

"I'm delighted to hear from you, Al. I assume everything went well."

There was a pause, then, "Not exactly."

A trickle of disturbance ran down Calhoun's innards and stopped somewhere in his bowels. "What do you mean, not exactly?"

"I mean that Mr. Barrington had better security than I had bargained for."

"Explain that, please."

"I mean that after assessing the situation and making a perfect plan, my plan turned out to be imperfect. I was confronted, disarmed, and dismissed from the country."

"By whom?"

"He didn't mention his name, but he was pointing a 30.06 deer rifle at my head. I was allowed to leave the country in one piece."

"Al, I paid you fifty thousand dollars and expenses to take care of this."

"And I will refund your money, every cent of it, immediately. Give me an address, and I will have it hand-delivered tomorrow."

"I'm about to leave the country — I'm on an airplane that is taxiing as we speak."

"No matter. I'll get the cash to you wherever you land."

"Can you get it to Rio, ah, undisturbed?"

"I can. Just give me an address."

Calhoun gave him the address of his apartment. "Don't leave it at the desk — come upstairs. I'll tell them to expect you."

"Fine."

"What name will you use?"

"Mr. Jones."

"Call me from the Rio airport."

"Right."

"When will you arrive?"

"In a day or two. I have arrangements to make."

"I'll expect you. Don't disappoint me."

"I try never to disappoint."

"Except this time."

"Except this time." Al hung up, stinging with embarrassment. He had never had to apologize to a client.

Calhoun hung up.

"What was that about?" Cheree asked.

"Nothing much — just a delivery of more cash to the Rio apartment."

The aircraft taxied onto the runway, and they were pressed into their seats by the acceleration on takeoff.

"There," Calhoun said when the landing gear came up. "We're off." He raised his glass of champagne. "Better times," he toasted.

"God, I'll drink to that," Cheree said.

Al began making phone calls: flight, transportation, tools.

57

At Windward Hall, a wrap party for the film was held, as other guests began arriving for a double wedding. Peter and Hattie would take their vows standing next to Ben and Tessa, his English girlfriend.

The redecoration of Curtis House had been completed by Susan's crews, working two shifts a day, and staff had been hired or imported from other Arrington hotels to man the place. It would be a good trial run for the new country house hotel.

Windward Hall rooms were occupied by members of the wedding party, and they filled out the cast and crew of the film for the wrap festivities.

Al got off an airplane in Rio after a night flight, and a car awaited him at the curb, driven by a man who handed him a brief-case. Al gave him the address of the apartment house, then opened the briefcase and examined its contents. The drive took a little less than an hour. On the way, Al phoned Calhoun.

"Yes?"

"It's Al. I'll be there shortly. Please let the reception people know."

"I'll look forward to seeing you. Did you bring me something?"

"Everything," Al said. He hung up and took a plastic envelope from his bag, containing a thick mustache, a bottle of glue, and a pair of black horn-rimmed glasses with Al's prescription. He applied the mustache, put on the glasses, and examined the result in the rear-seat vanity mirror. Better than good enough, he thought.

Peter stood on a chair and made a slightly tipsy speech to his people, and champagne glasses were raised by all.

The car pulled up half a block short of Calhoun's building; Al got out and strode into the lobby carrying the briefcase. "Dr. Calhoun is expecting me," he said to the man at the desk without slowing down. No one stopped him as he got onto the elevator and pressed the button for the penthouse.

Al got off the elevator to find Calhoun and his wife waiting for him in the foyer, next to a table holding a large flower arrangement. He hadn't counted on the wife, but what the hell?

"Al," Calhoun said, spreading his hands in welcome. "What have you brought me? And hey, I like the mustache."

Al shook the man's hand, then set the briefcase on the table and opened it. He took out the silenced pistol and, in one motion, pointed it at Calhoun's forehead and squeezed off a round. The wife was too shocked to move, and before she could speak, Al shot her in the same manner. He put the pistol back into the briefcase and turned to walk out. On second thought, he set the case back on the table and removed the pistol. Calhoun had not come here empty-handed, he figured. He walked quickly from room to room. No servants, that was good. And then, in the master bedroom, he found the rolling suitcase. He set it on the bed and unzipped it, then fell back as if struck. He had never seen so much cash in one place.

Al didn't bother to count it. He zipped it shut, then returned to the foyer, put the gun back into the case, and pressed the button for the elevator. It had not moved, so he stepped aboard and pressed the button for the lobby. The elevator fell as if the cable had broken, then, seconds later, opened into the lobby. Al strode across the space, looking neither to his left nor to his right, and left the building, carrying the briefcase and towing the suitcase. The car was still where he had left it no more than ten minutes before, and he got into the rear seat and set his luggage beside him. "Back to the airport. Departure terminal," he said to the driver while checking his watch. Two hours before his return flight.

Al opened the briefcase and wiped down every part of the pistol and the case, then he partly unzipped the suitcase and removed two small stacks of the hundred-dollar bills inside. As they rolled to a stop at the airport Al handed the driver a stack of bills. "For your trouble," he said, then he got out, leaving the briefcase on the backseat, and, declining a porter's help, he strode into the airport. As he waited in line at security he checked out the help there and picked his man. Late fifties, portly, tired-looking.

When his turn came he approached the man and showed him the stack of bills in his palm. "No X-ray, okay?" He slipped the stack into the man's hands.

"Arms out," the man said. He thumbed off the switch on the wand he held and made a show of moving around Al's body with the disabled wand. "Go ahead," the man said, winking.

Al didn't think the money would violate any laws, but he was glad he hadn't taken the chance. He pocketed the mustache, cleared immigration, walked to the first-class lounge, took a seat, and ordered a big breakfast. When his flight was called he was among the first aboard and quickly stowed his carry-on in the compartment across the aisle, where he could see it. He accepted a mimosa and settled in for the flight.

As Al's airplane took off a maid entered the Calhoun penthouse with her passkey, saw the two corpses on the floor in a large pool of mingled blood, and fainted. Her colleague found her a moment later and called the front desk, her hand trembling as she dialed the number.

Stone got to bed late, a little drunk, and felt the spot next to him for Susan. She wasn't there.

58

Stone was awakened by the telephone at midmorning. He fumbled for it. "Yes?"

"Stone, it's Lady Bourne. I thought you should know that Sir Charles appears to be slipping away. His doctor doesn't believe he'll last out the day."

"Thank you for telling me," Stone said. "I know this has been a difficult period for you, and I hope the future will be better. Would it be all right if I visited him?"

"I'm afraid he is unconscious — has been since the day before yesterday, so it wouldn't do either of you any good."

"I wish there were something I could do. Will you let me know if you think of anything?"

"I will, thank you." She hung up.

Stone went into his bathroom, shaved, showered, and began to dress. He took a shirt from the cabinet where they were stacked, shook it out, and got into it.

Something was wrong. It was a familiar shirt; he had had several of the same pattern made at Turnbull & Asser over the years, but this one didn't fit. The sleeves were too long, and it was tight around the middle. He took it off and inspected it. At the bottom of the shirt he found a label with a name on it, but it wasn't his. Sir Charles Bourne. The laundress must have mixed it in with his shirts, which wasn't surprising, since they both had the same maker's label.

He was about to refold it and return it to the laundress when he saw something that stopped him. The three buttonholes on the cuff were encrusted with what appeared to be dried blood, and there was a noticeable stain on the cuff itself. It was the sort of thing that would have stopped him in his tracks when he had been a homicide detective. He immediately began to imagine how the stain had got there.

Putting a bloody shirt into a washing machine with hot water would set, not remove, the stain. Blood had to be rinsed away with cold water before washing it in hot. If a man, say a former Royal Marine commando, wanted to kill a man with a knife, he would do it the way he had been trained. Approaching from behind, a right-handed man would clap his left hand over the victim's mouth, then, with his right hand, reach around and bring the knife blade across the throat, releasing a spurt of arterial blood that might well stain his left cuff. Stone was looking at the left cuff.

He went and sat on the bed and thought about this. What he had imagined was how the brigadier, a former Royal Marine commando, would have killed Sir Richard Curtis. But this shirt had not belonged to the brigadier, who was a smallish man; it had belonged to Charles Bourne, who was tall, and he had no doubt that DNA analysis would reveal the blood to be Sir Richard's. He believed he had just solved a murder.

He found another shirt and got dressed, then he telephoned Deputy Chief Inspector Holmes and invited him to the house for morning coffee. "I have something to show you," he said. Holmes accepted his invitation.

Stone had finished breakfast when Holmes arrived. The two men greeted each other cordially and sat down while coffee was brought.

"Thank you for coming, Inspector," Stone said. "There's something I have to show you." He handed the inspector the shirt. "Please examine the left cuff and tell me what you see."

Holmes looked at it. "I see a bloodstain that laundering did not wash away," he said. "I suppose it was washed in hot water."

"That is what I see, too, and I believe that analysis will prove it to be the blood of Sir Richard Curtis. Look at the small label at the bottom front of the shirt."

Holmes did so. "You are telling me that Sir Richard Curtis was murdered by Sir Charles Bourne and not the brigadier?"

"That is correct."

"The problem is, I have a written confession from the brigadier, expressing sorrow for what he had done."

"I think his sorrow arose from guilt," Stone said, "but not guilt over having murdered Sir Richard."

"Then what?"

"I believed, and I think you did, too, that Sir Charles had thought for many years that Sir Richard had had a continuing affair with Lady Bourne, and had fathered both her children."

"I think that is certainly a credible theory, based on the blood groups of the father and the two children."

"But the brigadier also had the same blood type."

"Yes, that is so. Are you saying that it was

the brigadier who fathered the two children?"

"I believe that to be the case."

"But Sir Charles believed Sir Richard to be the father."

"Yes, and that belief finally got the better of Sir Charles, and after an argument of some sort, he killed Sir Richard."

"And the brigadier's confession?"

"He was expressing guilt over having been the cause of Sir Richard's death. By not revealing to Sir Charles that he knew himself to be the father, he had allowed the killing to happen." Stone was beginning to feel that he was living in an Agatha Christie novel.

Holmes thought about it. "I believe that is a perfect solution to what happened, and if it is, the blood on Sir Charles's shirt should confirm it."

"I believe it will."

"And how did you come by the shirt?"

"Sir Charles and I have the same shirtmaker and the same laundress. I believe the laundress on the estate accidentally put his shirt in with mine and delivered them to me."

"Well, then," Holmes said, "I have a couple of jobs ahead of me: first, I must have the blood on the shirt analyzed, and if it proves your theory, I must then arrest Sir

Charles on a charge of murder."

"I'm afraid it's a bit too late for that," Stone said.

"How so?"

"Sir Charles lies, dying, a quarter of a mile from where we sit. His doctor believes he will not live out the day."

Holmes allowed himself a chuckle. "Then what would be the point of charging him?"

"I can't think of one. The brigadier is dead and has left no family, save his two natural children, who don't know he is their biological father. And Sir Charles is departing this life as we speak."

"Then you are suggesting that I — what's the expression? Let sleeping dogs lie?"

"What would be the point of doing anything else?"

"Well," Holmes said, rising, "I don't believe that is properly my decision to make. I am bound to take this shirt and this theory to my chief inspector. We will see what he has to say."

"Then do what you must," Stone said. "However, I don't think you are ethically bound to speak to him today. Perhaps tomorrow would do as well."

"You have a point, Mr. Barrington," Holmes said. "I'll make an appointment to see him tomorrow. I'm sure he's too busy to see me today."

The two men shook hands, and the deputy chief inspector took his leave, the shirt tucked into his raincoat pocket.

59

Stone lingered over a second cup of coffee after the inspector's departure, and he was shortly joined by Billy Barnett, who poured himself a cup and sat down.

"I have news," Billy said, handing Stone a copy of the *International New York Times,* open to page seven.

Stone picked up the newspaper and read the headline:

TV EVANGELIST & WIFE DIE IN RIO SHOOTING

He read on:

Dr. Don Beverly Calhoun, a television evangelist, was found in his Rio de Janeiro penthouse apartment, along with his wife, Cheree, both shot to death. Police said he had been expecting a visitor, who went up to the apartment then left again minutes before a housemaid discovered the bodies. The man was described as heavyset, tall, and with a mustache and horn-rimmed glasses. He was not seen again after leaving the building, and a search is under way for him. The motive was thought to be robbery, but as yet nothing has been found missing from the apartment.

"Sounds like our visitor," Stone said.

"Doesn't it? Bar the mustache, of course."

"Did you have any involvement in this, Billy?"

Billy did not answer the question directly. "My theory is that Dr. Don, on learning that Al Junior had failed in his mission, demanded his money back. Al probably believed that a better way to settle the debt was to eliminate the debt holder."

Stone nodded. "Makes sense. I seem to remember that Dino told me that the police, when they searched Dr. Don's New York apartment, found a large sum of cash in his safe."

"I remember that, too — eight hundred thousand, wasn't it?"

"I believe so."

"The article mentions that nothing was found missing from the apartment, but it fails to mention anything being found, either."

"Are the police looking for Al Junior?"

"I don't see why they should. I haven't heard anyone mention a connection between him and Dr. Don. Also, it's well known that the United States and Brazil do not have an extradition treaty, and that works both ways."

"Is Al Junior any kind of threat to us?"

"I don't think so. Al Junior works under contract, and he no longer has an employer with any interest in you or yours."

"Well, as far as I'm concerned, whoever assisted Dr. Don into the next life has done the world a favor," Stone said.

"I tend to agree. Let's just leave it at that."

"Agreed. What are your plans now that you've wrapped the film?"

"I suppose we'll all go back to L.A. shortly. I understand from Peter that Ben and Centurion Studios are having talks about his replacing the retiring CEO as head of the studio."

"Then I'm glad Peter has you to back him up."

"And I'm glad to be able to help him. I find the work very satisfying. What are your plans?"

"I think I'm going to have to get back to

New York and repair some bridges with Woodman & Weld, who seem to think I have spent too much time here of late."

"It's nice to be needed," Billy observed.

"That remains to be seen," Stone replied. "I like it here so much that I'm afraid New York won't satisfy me the way it always has."

"Do I detect a midlife crisis in the offing?"

"That remains to be seen," Stone said. "Dino and Viv are returning for the wedding, and when that's over, we'll all be on our way back."

"And Susan Blackburn?"

"She can't be parted from her expanding business."

"Oh, well."

"Oh, well, indeed."

60

Rain fell hard on the roof of the country church, and its pews were full, with others standing at the rear, as last services were conducted for Sir Charles Bourne. As the service ended, the rain stopped and sunshine began to pour through the stained-glass windows.

The grave had been sheltered from the storm by a tent, and this was taken away as the crowd assembled at the burial site. Another short ceremony was conducted, along with a final prayer, and the pallbearers lowered the coffin into its receptacle.

As the crowd lined up to offer their condolences to the widow, then drifted back toward the car park, Stone saw Lady Bourne in conversation with Deputy Chief Inspector Holmes. He tipped his hat and left her to deal with the last mourners.

Stone caught up with the policeman in the car park. "Did Lady Bourne have anything new to say to you?" he asked.

"There was a deathbed confession," Holmes replied. "Your theory was confirmed."

"Is there anything else to be done?"

"No, I don't think so. My chief inspector will feel the same way, I think. I understand you've a wedding this evening."

"That's correct — a double wedding, actually."

"Then please offer my best wishes to the four of them."

"I will do that."

The two men shook hands, and Holmes drove away.

The ceremony took place in the great hall at Curtis House, officiated by two priests, an Anglican and a Catholic. Close to forty guests had arrived from London and the States.

Stone stood with Dino and Viv, plus Mary Ann Bacchetti, Ben's mother. "They're a handsome group, aren't they?" Mary Ann observed of the crowd. "They all look right out of Central Casting as a Hollywood crowd."

"And none handsomer than the celebrants," Dino added.

"Isn't this where the brides and grooms

are supposed to make their escapes for their respective honeymoons?" Viv asked.

"There's a Centurion Studios Gulfstream waiting for them at the airstrip," Stone said. "They'll sleep in Cannes tonight. After the honeymoon, the airplane will come back here to pick up a few others of the crew, then fly them all, nonstop, back to Los Angeles."

"And when are you all going back?" Mary Ann asked.

"Tomorrow morning, in my airplane. May we give you a lift back to New York?"

"Thank you, but I'm spending a few days in London with friends, as long as I'm on this side of the pond. Can your airplane make the trip nonstop?"

"No, we'll stop for fuel at Santa Maria, in the Azores, then again at St. John's, Newfoundland, thence to Teterboro."

There was a move of the crowd toward the front door, to wave off the happy couples, then the party resumed without them.

The following morning their luggage was loaded aboard the Citation CJ3 Plus, and Stone ran through his checklists, then taxied to the end of the runway and took off. Turning west, with the sun at their backs, the light jet climbed to forty thousand feet and was cleared on course to Santa Maria.

Late that night, tired from his long flight, Stone slept in his own New York bed. Once, he had to get up and he was disoriented, thinking he was still at Windward House.

By tomorrow morning he would have made the adjustment, except for the jet lag.

He already missed England.

AUTHOR'S NOTE

I am happy to hear from readers, but you should know that if you write to me in care of my publisher, three to six months will pass before I receive your letter, and when it finally arrives it will be one among many, and I will not be able to reply.

However, if you have access to the Internet, you may visit my website at www.stuartwoods.com, where there is a button for sending me e-mail. So far, I have been able to reply to all my e-mail, and I will continue to try to do so.

If you send me an e-mail and do not receive a reply, it is probably because you are among an alarming number of people who have entered their e-mail address incorrectly in their mail software. I have many of my replies returned as undeliverable.

Remember: e-mail, reply; snail mail, no reply.

When you e-mail, please do not send attachments, as I never open these. They can take twenty minutes to download, and they often contain viruses.

Please do not place me on your mailing lists for funny stories, prayers, political causes, charitable fund-raising, petitions, or sentimental claptrap. I get enough of that from people I already know. Generally speaking, when I get e-mail addressed to a large number of people, I immediately delete it without reading it.

Please do not send me your ideas for a book, as I have a policy of writing only what I myself invent. If you send me story ideas, I will immediately delete them without reading them. If you have a good idea for a book, write it yourself, but I will not be able to advise you on how to get it published. Buy a copy of *Writer's Market* at any bookstore; that will tell you how.

Anyone with a request concerning events or appearances may e-mail it to me or send it to: Publicity Department, Penguin Random House LLC, 375 Hudson Street, New York, NY 10014.

Those ambitious folk who wish to buy film, dramatic, or television rights to my books should contact Matthew Snyder, Creative Artists Agency, 9830 Wilshire Boulevard, Beverly Hills, CA 98212-1825.

Those who wish to make offers for rights of a literary nature should contact Anne Sibbald, Janklow & Nesbit, 445 Park Avenue, New York, NY 10022. (Note: This is not an invitation for you to send her your manuscript or to solicit her to be your agent.)

If you want to know if I will be signing books in your city, please visit my website, www.stuartwoods.com, where the tour schedule will be published a month or so in advance. If you wish me to do a book signing in your locality, ask your favorite bookseller to contact his Penguin representative or the Penguin publicity department with the request.

If you find typographical or editorial errors in my book and feel an irresistible urge to tell someone, please write to Sara Minnich at Penguin's address above. Do not e-mail your discoveries to me, as I will already have learned about them from others.

A list of my published works appears on my website. All the novels are still in print in paperback and can be found at or ordered from any bookstore. If you wish to obtain hardcover copies of earlier novels or of the two nonfiction books, a good used-book store or one of the online bookstores can help you find them. Otherwise, you will have to go to a great many garage sales.

ABOUT THE AUTHOR

Stuart Woods is the author of more than sixty novels, including the *New York Times*-bestselling Stone Barrington and Holly Barker series. He is a native of Georgia and began his writing career in the advertising industry. *Chiefs,* his debut in 1981, won the Edgar Award. An avid sailor and pilot, Woods lives in Florida, Maine, and New Mexico.

stuartwoods.com
facebook.com/StuartWoodsAuthor